ONE LAST CRUISE

A COLLECTION OF SHORT STORIES

By Luke McEwen

This is a work of fiction. Names, characters, places and
incidents either are products of the author's imagination or
are used fictitiously. Any resemblance to actual events or
locales or persons, living or dead, is entirely coincidental.

Published by Unchained Pen Ltd

A CIP catalogue record for this book is available from
the British Library.

ISBN:978-1-910304-00-6 Paperback
ISBN:978-1-910304-01-3 Electronic Book

DEDICATION

My father had a wonderful career as a journalist. He now runs an English language school in Italy and he has plans to publish a book on learning to speak English. My great grandfather wrote books on social history and about his career as a solicitor. Writing must be in the genes. So thank you Dad for those genes and most of all for your love and encouragement.

ACKNOWLEDGEMENTS

Editor: Kate McMahon.   Thank you Kate for your professionalism and encouragement.

Photography: The Thimble: Kate Smith
                Through the Eyes of Medusa: Toby McEwen.

Medical consultant: One Last Cruise: Cristina Lipan

Life wisdom: Nathalie Petite

TABLE OF CONTENTS

One Last Cruise

While one finds company in himself and his pursuits, he cannot feel old, no matter what his years may be.

Amos Bronson Alcott

Chapter One

"Happy eighty-first, darling," Tilly said as she kissed Bert on his slumbering cheek. "I'll get your birthday treat. Do you want the radio on?"

Bert's face was as dormant as it was wrinkled but it suddenly sprung into life. "I'll just snooze some more, Tilly-Snugs. I'm dancing in the 'Strictly' final. You and I are glorious!"

"OK, dear, make sure you give a good acceptance speech." She adjusted the curtains to block a sunbeam that was threatening to disturb his dancing. "Don't forget to tell everyone you owe your deepest gratitude to your darling wife," she giggled.

As Bert heard the door close he brought his dream to an abrupt end. He magnanimously deferred to the younger couple. They needed the limelight more than Tilly and he.

He reached for the box file that he'd stashed under the bed and went straight to the page that he had been looking at last night. Bert studied the itinerary. Did it or did it not include Antigua? And did the ship have live entertainment every night, which were the shows that they had loved so much? The box file heaved with brochures, travel notes, Caribbean travel guides, the start of their shopping list, vaccination requirements and a packing list. He had been busy.

Tilly called from the kitchen, "Will you please try the wholegrain?" Bert broke off from his studies and contemplated the thought of the rustic, dry bread.

"It's my birthday, Tilly-Snugs. White, two slices, and two eggs, please." He picked up the brochure again. "Can you put the salt cellar on the tray plea-se?"

Bert enjoyed elongating the sound of the word 'please'.

Tilly frowned as she began to dutifully line up Bert's medication. Since his heart attack he had used a large variety of drugs to reduce his blood pressure and support a regular rhythm. Sometimes she would ignore the pill box and set his tablets out in a pretty pattern. Today, being Bert's birthday, she laid them on his toast in a heart shape. They looked quite colourful: the blue ACE inhibitor, the titanium-white nitrates, the pink blood-thinner and the bronze water pill, as well as the olive-green magnesium and red potassium supplements.

Bert took Clopidogrel to thin his blood, either in combination with aspirin or sometimes with a thrombolytic, a drug that dissolved blood clots. The nitrates let his veins and arteries relax. The ACE inhibitor decreased the tension in his blood vessels and blood volume, thus lowering his blood pressure. The diuretic, commonly known as a 'water pill', helped prevent fluid buildup in his body. In addition to these drugs he took magnesium and potassium supplements once a day. All these meds usually caused liver problems so he also took cholesterol medication, ZOCOR, which is a lipid-lowering agent. To help that do its work more efficiently he took fibre pills and omega-3 capsules once a day.

Bert grabbed his pen to jot down the idea that he'd had in the night. If he brought the holiday forward to February it would be Tilly's birthday. He contemplated the special arrangements he could organize. He could ask the entertainment staff to sing 'Happy Birthday' to her in the evening, or perhaps they could order room service!

She would be eighty. "Octogenarians," he said aloud. What a lovely word. Only another nine years left to refer to himself as that. What would he be then? A nonagenarian. That didn't have quite the same ring.

Tilly was at the door. Bert quickly buried the box file and notes under the duvet.

"What have you got there, Albert?" She peered at him over her glasses as her foot battled with the door. She nimbly manoeuvered the full breakfast tray through the doorway. "Not porn? You've got the digits back to front! You're eighty-one, not eighteen!"

"Just a bit of light reading material dear, with some colourful pictures. It's the pictures which are the most titillating!" He grinned at her.

"Where did you get it?" She imagined her husband thumbing through the magazines on the top shelf at the corner store, *how embarrassing*! "Oh, Albert! Really?! What is it? Playboy or something?"

Bert didn't answer. He sat with his lips pursed, impersonating a prisoner under interrogation. Tilly passed him the tray as she climbed in. She saw that she wasn't going to get a reply and began investigating with her hand.

"Ooh, Tilly-Snugs, I know it's my birthday...!" Bert chuckled.

"Albert, what have you been up to?" She pulled out the travel brochure and examined its glossy cover. She stared at him in disbelief.

"Just a few thoughts, dear."

Tilly sighed, "It's ridiculous! We've been here before, all booked up and then cancelled. No one wants to insure us! Bert, we're just not well enough to travel, and that's that."

He balanced his breakfast tray on his lap. The thought of cancelling his travel plans made the bacon unappealing. He felt the box file under his knees, now an object of redundancy not adventure.

"I did find a cruise that visits that beach you love. You know, the one where you fell in love with that American billionaire. I fell in love with him too, especially his wallet!" Bert poked a finger beneath her arm, but she didn't laugh.

"He was very debonair, as I recall, a very charming man," Tilly protested.

"An affair with a debonair billionaire, how romantic!" Bert put on his posh voice and raised an eyebrow. "He bought you a drink."

"He bought us both a drink! Don't give me that, Albert!" She poked him back.

"So what do you say then, dear, one more cruise?"

"Bert, come on. A cruise would be madness. No one's going to take us. Remember the last time? We nearly didn't get our money back!"

"That was the heart attack, over three years ago now!"

"No one will give us insurance. You remember the form? 'Has your doctor advised you not to travel?'"

"Well, that was our mistake. If we hadn't asked him we could have gone. We wouldn't have failed that stupid form. If we don't ask the doctor then he can't advise us not to travel!"

"Bert!"

"Tilly-Bum!" He tickled her once more.

"No, Bert." She pushed his hand gently away. "This isn't a game. If we get ill then our insurance is invalid. And we'd have to sell the house to pay the medical bills. What about the kids' inheritance?"

"Bugger their inheritance. They don't need it anyway!"

"That's hardly the point."

"It is the point, it's the whole point!"

"What if we died? The kids would have to fly over,

5

pay all our medical bills and then pay to get us back to England. Perhaps in a wooden box on a plane." She gave him a hard stare over her glasses.

They sat in silence until Bert sighed heavily. "We never lived like this when we were young. We always chased our dreams."

"Yes, but we're not young anymore!" Tilly took a deep breath, letting the air flow slowly out. "I know it's irritating, but we've got to live within our abilities. We're not forty anymore."

"And neither are we dead!" He grimaced, struggling to find the words he needed. "We've given up so much: cake, biscuits, chips — Christ — the doctor even told me to give up chess! It's too stressful for my heart. When did we last make love, or dance even? It's just too much, Tilly!" He looked at her, mouth open. "We've always done the things we've wanted and done them our way. That was how we brought up Nathalie and Craig, why should it change now? What's left? I'm not just going to hang around and wait for the box to arrive. We are still alive!" Bert threw the holiday brochure on the floor. "I can't give it all up!" He swung his legs out of the bed and stood up, not looking at his wife.

"Bert? Bert! Things have changed. We aren't who we used to be. I need a new hip, my angina is always threatening to keep me in the chair and you can't do what you used to do!"

"We've always followed our hearts."

"You make it sound like it's my fault. Bert!?" Tilly looked at her husband, and waited for his answer.

He remembered it was his birthday and felt bad that he'd started the day off in a huff. "OK, dear, we'll leave it. I know you're right. It was just a whim." He turned and nodded. "Think nothing of it."

*

Tilly sat on the bed alone. Bert was busy with his morning routine, which included walking to the corner shop to collect a pint of milk and the paper. The ten-minute walk, that had started twenty years ago, had now stretched to half an hour. There was only one crossing to worry about, but he was good at waving the traffic down so he could cross. Just lately he had started to take a few minutes' break at the halfway mark. Sometimes strangers would stop to chat. They would often show their concern and he had fun counting the amount of times that a mobility scooter was suggested.

Tilly thought of Bert's face when he had left. She couldn't get him to smile at her. That wasn't like him. She decided to start her morning chores and began with making the bed. As Tilly pulled back the eiderdown she saw Bert's box of holiday planning. She picked through his papers and saw his notes on best dates, favorite destinations, cruise ships and alternatives for excursions. *Not so much of a whim then*! she thought.

As Tilly gave the lounge a quick hoover, she decided it was time to give their dance trophy cups a quick dust. It was an impressive display. They had been enthusiastic all-round dancers, mastering the tango, rumba, quickstep, waltz and many more. They had loved the weekly routine: learning the new dance moves, travelling to the various dance halls across the country, meeting new people, out-competing those people and then, hopefully, bringing back the trophies, both for the pride of the club as well as their own joy. They had met so many people through dancing. When they finally gave up the competitions they began to teach, and Bert had earned a good reputation. Students would come from outside the county for a lesson. But above all, dancing had brought them happiness. It was how they had met.

Bert had asked Tilly to partner him in a competition. He had her laughing at every moment of the event and to top it all off, they'd won. Many years later he had admitted that the dance competition was a ruse to win her heart. People complimented them on how good they were together: dancing as one person, totally in sync, totally at ease and totally in their element. That was the magic that had brought them so much success. Bert had said that dancing was, 'Life itself, moving to the rhythm and feeling the melody'. He could switch off all his troubles and just concentrate on the things that brought him adventure, excitement, praise, success and joy.

As Tilly wiped a feather duster over the centerpiece of the display - a gold plated cup nearly a foot tall - she recalled Bert's face when he had received it. It seemed that victory had kept a smile on his face for the whole year. But they hadn't danced for years now. He needed something else.

"Never live without a dream in mind, that's what we promised each other."

Tilly looked up to see Bert had been watching her. His expression was a curious mixture of sullen despondence and suffering hope.

She looked at the dance cup and then to Bert. "OK," she smiled, "one last cruise."

*

The next day Bert and Tilly sat in front of Deborah, who sat behind a tidy desk. This was a different travel agent from last time. It had meant a twenty-minute bus ride, but they weren't known here, and neither was their medical history. Tilly had sworn her husband to silence when it came to answering any questions relating to their health.

Deborah was one in a long line of seven. Bert's box file had been spread over her workspace and she had smiled politely as he enthused on his meticulous plans.

"And I'm guessing you'd prefer a cruise without any young children?"

"Oh no, we don't mind a few young children." Bert didn't need to look to Tilly for agreement.

"They can be quite entertaining," Tilly contributed.

"Especially watching the parents' attempts to contain them," Bert chuckled. "Do you have children, Debbie?"

"Albert, she's a Deborah," Tilly corrected.

"Yes I do, two little ones, in years four and five."

Bert realised that 'years four and five' referred to school years but couldn't remember what that meant. He concluded that they must be very young.

"Ooh, do you have a picture?" Tilly asked.

Deborah turned the photo frame around on her desk.

"They're good lookers, Deborah, just like their mother!" Bert played with the sound of her name, extending the length of 'borah'.

Deborah blushed and busied herself with her computer screen. "And will you be wanting a balcony?"

"I don't think so, we don't plan to spend much time in the cabin," Tilly answered, "I think we'd be quite happy with an inside cabin too, if it means we can save a bob."

"Very wise, madam. And can we help you with your medical insurance? Can we sort that out at the same time and save you the trouble of coming back?"

Tilly quickly squeezed Bert's hand. This was her question. "Yes please, let's do that."

"OK, let me just put some details in and we can do a quote. So it's just for the two of you?"

"Just the two of us, unless you'd like to come with us?" Bert chuckled.

"Bert, be good! Yes please."

"Can I just get your dates of birth?"

"Bert's is the twenty-eighth of August 1932 and mine is the ninth of November 1939."

"Tilly's the baby," he chuckled.

Deborah looked at the monitor screen. Their hearts tightened. Tilly wasn't sure if it was her angina. Both tried to stay calm. "So you're eighty-one, Mr. Wadehurst?" He nodded, forcing a wide smile. "Right. OK. There are usually some special questions I need to ask for that."

"Nice to be special." Bert felt his hand being squeezed as a caution. He threw a smile at Tilly.

Deborah read aloud, "Have either of you suffered from or received any ongoing treatment for any heart or cancer condition in the last five years?"

"No." Tilly's 'no' was robotic. She looked down at the table, focusing on Deborah moving her mouse.

"Currently receiving or have you received in the last twelve months, any advice, medication or treatment for any illness, injury or disease?" Bert bit his lip; he wanted to make a joke about venereal disease, but knew it would be a joke too far.

"No." Tilly subconsciously leant her head on her hand, covering up the scar from her thyroid cancer.

"Under investigation or awaiting results for any diagnosed or undiagnosed medical condition?" Bert managed to not talk about possible Tourettes.

"No."

"Travelling against your UK doctor's advice, or for the purpose of obtaining treatment?" Bert looked at

Tilly. For this one she would be OK.

"No." Tilly managed to look up and smile at Deborah.

"Received a terminal prognosis?" Bert tried hard to switch off.

"No."

"Last one, sorry. On a waiting list for, or aware of the need for, any in-patient treatment?"

"No."

"That's great, that should work out fine. We had a horrible situation last month, where the quote came out at over a thousand pounds per person; they needed to follow it up with extra evidence and everything. They almost weren't allowed to go."

"Really! That's awful." Tilly continued to calm herself as she pushed away the image of the cruise ship having to turn around because her angina was too severe.

"OK, it's come back with a price of one hundred and eighty pounds, but that is for the both of you." Deborah looked up. "I know it seems a lot but…"

"That's fine, it's about the same as the other quote we had," Tilly reassured her. "You can just add that on to the cost of the cruise, can you?"

"Yes of course." Deborah visibly relaxed. Her morning's work had not been scuppered.

"Should I have mentioned about my prostate, Debbie?" Bert's serious face cracked. "Just kidding Deborah." Neither Tilly nor Deborah laughed, but grimaced in relief.

Chapter Two

It was a dreamy start to their dream holiday. There was only one point of stress, when Tilly had had to explain to customs why her handbag was so full of drugs. She had tried to charm the young official, complimenting him on his lovely smile and explained that the drugs were precautionary. The official had looked at her without expression or smile and merely pushed the bag back towards her.

Tilly had decided not to leave any medication in their suitcases to avoid the problems that would be created if their luggage were to be lost in the system. Arriving in the Caribbean for a week and not having their medication would have been a disaster. She had also decided to get spares for all the drugs so that Bert could carry them in his hand luggage too. In order to get an extra prescription she had said that their medicine cabinet had been waterlogged.

Her medicine regime was as complicated as Bert's. The Levothroid that she took once daily, one hour before breakfast, replaced what her thyroid had once done before it had been removed. The cancer had given her type 1 diabetes and this meant insulin injections fifteen minutes before each meal.

For the rheumatoid arthritis she took non-steroidal anti-inflammatory drugs, ibuprofen, as the Diclofenac gave her wind. She took this three times a day and it needed to be proceeded with a gastro protective pill, Ranitidine, fifteen minutes before the ibuprofen. There was also the Rheumatrex, which she had to take every twelve hours. It was effective but often it gave her a mouth ulcer or an itchy rash. Fortunately, the Humira could be left at home as that only had to be taken every other week.

The anxiety of customs could now all be forgotten, for they had arrived. The Caribbean heat, the wonderful blue skies, the adventure of entering the boat and all the thousands of people – it was everything they needed to feel like they were in heaven. They were so lucky to be there.

They had dressed for dinner in their formal wear; it had been a long time since they had done that. Bert's DJ was looking a little out of fashion now compared to the younger passengers, but Tilly liked the old-style better. The new designs looked lackluster and plain. It was the part of the cruise that they enjoyed the most: the grandeur and formality of dinner. In the past, if you were in a small party most cruises tended to arrange a table of fellow passengers for you to sit with, most often in parties of three or four couples. You tended to stay with the same people for the whole week, so one would get to know them well. On previous cruises Tilly and Bert had remained in touch with these fellow passengers for years afterward.

Time had brought a change to this little tradition. Now cruise ships often catered for buffet-style twenty-four hour eating, with an informal dress code. This ship had a combination of the two and Tilly and Bert had opted for traditional. They had been seated with Graham and Melanie from Surrey. Graham was a banker and Melanie was starting a small business as they patiently tried for a baby. Craig and Susan were also on their table. Craig was in finance; no one really understood what he did. His wife Susan, his P.A., was equally as enigmatic, although she seemed to share the same unease around the dinner table as Melanie. But Graham and Craig were at home with the occasion and, after the initial introductions and food orders had been placed, they had commanded the conversation with, firstly, an analysis of the current global economic climate and, secondly, a damning critique of the effect of the uncontrolled use of hedge funds dealing exclusively with intangibles. It was Craig who was most animated on the subject.

"What caused the crisis? Derivatives! Regulators and the media just won't admit it."

"Yeah, but…" Graham tried to start.

"It just doesn't add up. If you were to total the value of every stock on the planet, the entire market capitalization would be about thirty-seven trillion dollars. If you do the same process for bonds, right, you'd get a market capitalization of roughly seventy-three trillion dollars. Are you with me?" Graham stared, neither nodding nor giving an affirmation of his agreement. As he finally opened his mouth Craig continued, "Well the notional value of the derivative market is roughly one point four quadrillion dollars!"

Bert had once been in business, many years ago. He had been successful and had generated a good pension for them, but he had been successful not through his understanding of figures but through his engagement with the customers and the staff. He failed to understand what these young men were talking about. Was it him or was this just a tad tedious? "Melanie, I do love your pretty dress. Do you like these dinner parties on the cruise?" Bert spoke quietly, not wanting to interrupt the boys.

"Yes, but to be honest sometimes I could do with a pizza and some chips!"

"Me too, Melanie. Sounds like you're one of us. Are you into all this finance stuff?"

"No, that's Graham's lot. He loves it enough for the

both of us. I don't really understand what he's talking about half the time."

Tilly smiled. "Thank goodness – we were feeling like a pair of dummies. So, do you work, Melanie? You know, you do hold yourself so gracefully."

"I'm a physiotherapist, qualified for five years now. I try and do it as much as I can, but Graham likes me to be at home."

Bert couldn't resist. "Well, if Tilly was so good at massage I'd want her to be at home too."

"Albert, behave!"

"I must say, Melanie, you may be good with your hands but I love the way you talk, it's very melodic and tuneful. Melodic Melanie. Can I call you Melody?"

"So, you're Bert, is that right?" Graham had cut short his conversation with Craig.

"Yes, and this is my wife, Tilly. I'm afraid we were a bit lost in your talk about the economy."

"But you follow the news, don't you?"

"Oh yes, I always pay attention so I can identify what banker is responsible for destroying my pension!" Tilly, Melanie and Susan laughed freely. Graham and Craig eyed Bert seriously.

"It's not so clear cut. It's all quite complex when you look at the combination of economic cycle, subprime mortgages and the new derivative generation."

"Well, that's why we watch the 'One Show' – they make it so easy to understand. Some greedy bankers lent money to someone who wanted what they couldn't afford, for a bigger bonus they didn't really need. And then someone in charge got out their calculator and realised it didn't add up."

Tilly, Melanie and Susan tried very hard to disguise their mirth. Graham and Craig's frowns presented an interesting mirror of each other.

"As I said, it really is quite complex." Graham did his best to look nonchalant. "Waiter! Waiter! Yes, we ordered a bottle of red that hasn't arrived."

"Yes, sir," the waiter sheepishly nodded.

Bert was quickly in, "Ah, waiter?"

"Yes, Sir?"

"You're doing a fine job, well done!"

"Thank you, Sir."

Tilly stared at Bert. It was all that he needed to know that he should stop.

"Susan, it is Susan, isn't it?" Tilly broke the silence. "I heard you discussing the sailing excursion with the rep – did you get anywhere? Bert and I are trying to work out what it's all about."

It was the first time Susan had spoken and she spoke softly. "I think it starts about nine-thirty. No, wait, it's ten." As Susan spoke Tilly took out her pill box, and passed Bert his tablets. "It's an all-day thing. They provide food and apparently a non-stop rum punch," Susan smiled.

"Sounds lovely!"

Craig had been waiting to speak. "It's actually not bad value, when we did St Lucia last year they wanted thirty quid extra. I think it will be a great day out. The boat's not too big and I think the plan is to stop every hour to swim from the boat to the islands we pass. It's not a bad format."

Tilly continued to look at Susan. "He had lovely teeth, didn't he dear? Quite a handsome man!" Susan looked puzzled. "The rep! They always seem to pick the dishy ones."

"I've still got my own teeth, you know; look at these." Bert stretched out his cheeks to show his gold fillings, scattered amongst the yellow-brown teeth and dark gaps. "Still got my own hair too!"

"Bert, no one wants to see your teeth!"

The whole table laughed and he showed off his toothy grin again.

Chapter 3

Nick's head was heavy. Lifting it off the pillow took all his energy. *Who hit me?* he thought. Then he remembered the evening: too many Jagerbombs, too much Jack Daniels, too much coke, too many of the dancers and not enough sleep!

He heard the knocking. The knocking that had awoken him.

"Nick?" The voice came from the door. "Nick, the show! You need to get up."

Nick walked to the door, his eyes closed. He opened the door to find the DJ. "Nick, you arse, we're on in twenty-five. Get some clothes on! Oh and by the way, those aren't your pants."

Nick opened one eye and looked down at the pink knickers he was wearing. Were they Lisa's or Charlotte's?

Nick walked to the bathroom, closing his eyes as he turned on the light. The light, eventually allowed in, stung as it negotiated the adjustment of his pupils. He held himself on the sink for a moment. Was that the movement of the boat or had he left his body at last night's party?

His eyes finally parted and the mirror revealed the shell of a body and a face, which was somehow wearing a mask bearing similarities to his own. What was that crease underneath his eye? That was new. He looked hard at the face in the mirror.

The summer in Magaluf with the eighteen to thirty lot seemed so long ago. Getting the contract with this cruise company seemed like a blur. He struggled to remember how long he had been on the boat. How many times had he crossed the ocean? How many countries had he been to? Nick never got off the boat at the ports. It was a good opportunity to sleep whilst the boat was quiet. If he did venture ashore it was only to stock up with cheap booze and score some drugs. It was becoming increasingly difficult to buy them on the boat. The guy in engineering had been thrown off the ship some weeks ago.

He preferred his job on the ship to the repping with the eighteen to thirties crowd. You got a better class of punter on the ship: passengers with money, who would buy you champagne, had celebrity connections and interesting stories to tell. Birds with class, who had a bit of culture; who didn't just want to copulate like animals at every opportunity.

But of course, essentially, people were people. He was paid to make people laugh – a modern day jester. These punters were older and richer, but in the end it came down to the same thing: giving them an opportunity to forget about their real lives at home.

Nick began his morning ritual. It was so ingrained that it required no thought. He cut the powder in two. "Not too much, Nicky, just a light medication, nothing too heavy," he said aloud. He made the lines with his plastic card room key. "One for port and one for starboard," he said as he snuffled up the poison, which he knew would one day kill him. Dragging a wet finger over the remaining powder he rubbed it along his front gum.

He stared in the mirror, waiting for his eyes to focus on his own pupils.

"You are a beautiful man." He smiled and the coke helped him to interpret his reflection with whiter teeth and smoother skin.

"Let's get the show rocking!" His hand hovered

over the two different hairbrushes, one for his curly fringe and one for the long hair that he tied into a ponytail and pinned up.

"Right, you old posh gits, get off your fat arses and show me some respect. Time for a bit of ritual humiliation."

*

Nick tapped the microphone to address the audience. They were sat around the dance floor, on a mixture of sofas and brightly upholstered arm chairs. "Ladies and gentleman." Nick waited for the sound of chatter to fade. "Ladies and gentleman, good evening to you!" The audience failed to bid him the same, but finally the last of the babble hushed. "Those who came to the welcome meeting will remember my lovely assistant, Charlotte. And of course the lovely me, who goes by the name of Nicholas - because that's how I like to leave the ladies." His joke got a mixed reception, mostly embarrassed laughter. Nick groaned internally. The audiences in Magaluf had been so much easier. Back there, in twenty minutes, he would have had them out of control, fondling and shouting obscenities at each other.

Tilly and Bert had found their dinner companions and were sat on a lush velour sofa. Tilly appreciated the soft cushions. She was hopeful of a good show and some laughter before her plan came to fruition. She passed Bert the special pill from her purse.

"I don't recognise this one, dear. I don't remember a purple one!"

"It's a little something extra, a recommendation from Doctor Denning. He said you'd be all right with it, but not to mix it with the nitrates."

"Oh! Well, if that's what the doctor ordered…."

"It's for that holiday adventure you wanted."

Bert looked at Tilly, trying to understand. "This is the adventure I wanted, Tilly-Bum."

Nick walked to the centre of the empty stage, spread out his arms and held his head up to the spotlight. The audience began to quieten down in anticipation. "Ladies and gentlemen, chicks and dudes, tonight has begun!" Nick took a quick bow to the polite clapping. "OK, boys and girls, time for fun and laughter. We have a prize here, two tickets for tomorrow's Big Cat excursion, sailing around the small islands. There's music and rum punch all day long as you swim from the boat to the beautiful white sands of your fantasy, dream island." Nick held the tickets above his head. They were in fact just a pair of cocktail menus. Special tickets were never printed for excursions, but this was show business. "Now you can do anything, ladies and gents, but the competition will be judged by my own internal clap-o-meter, nothing to do with my herpes, but a wow-o-meter. That's it, guys, the couple that makes the audience give up the most noise, wins. I want the audience to clap if they recognise *sexy*. Raw, beautiful, romantic, scintillating sexiness."

The crowd looked horrified. A quiet hum of chatter ensued, "What did he say, 'sexy'? What are we supposed to do? Did he say 'pairs'?" Murmurs of confusion and personal anxiety escalated. The noise of passive resistance ensued.

In their little circle, Craig was the first to break. "Come on then, Graham – what are you going to do for us?"

Graham shrugged. "I came here for entertainment, not to *be* the entertainment."

Nick continued the pressure. "Come on, guys,

21

surely you have some sexiness in you, or has the sherry trifle and paté *foie gras* absorbed all your lustiness?"

The first of the defensive heckling came. "Come on then! You show us what you can do!" There was no fear in Nick's mind that he would die on stage. His ego was elevated due to unnatural substances. He was working with senses united and fired up on a gram of white magic; cultivated, processed and refined from one hundred coca leaves.

Nick could have chosen anyone from the audience, but as he sought to inspire his audience he spied Bethany by the bar, one of the ship's dancers. Nick brought his lips to the microphone, lowered his voice to several tones lower than his natural baritone, and gently pronounced, "Beth-an-y..." His voice sounded like a sinister demagogue calling from the underworld. He pointed to Bethany. "Your moment has come."

The audience looked across to the bar. Nick held back from his oratory, personally interested in what her response would be. Bethany, the 'petite curly blonde model, dancer, actress/extra and singer', as described by her online profile, smiled and placed her vodka and coke carefully on the bar. From thirty yards away, she appeared to engage Nick's stare and nodded her agreement to the challenge.

"Step right up, Bethany, and show these guys how it's done."

Bethany gracefully lowered herself from the bar stool, revealing her tightly-bodiced lace dress. Her hair was all fire and snakes. She walked like the last model on a catwalk, wearing the headline dress. The finest of the finest. One hundred and sixty guests watched as the nubile teenager, fresh from dance school, walked to Nick. In that moment eighty male fantasies were created, ranging from the pitiful to the ridiculous -

from, 'Can I have this dance,' to, 'Your cabin is damaged and unusable, you can share mine.'

Bethany stood in front of Nick, her hand on her waist and her left leg slightly forward, impersonating both Marilyn and Jessica all in one 'I got it, you want it' caricature.

The audience was glued. Nick's walk turned to a skip as he spied a free chair and collected it from a table. As he returned to Bethany he spun the chair around and sat on it, Christine Keeler-style. "OK, Bethany, you know the rules, biggest noise wins, it's all about *sexiness*. Plant one on me!"

A whisper rose from the audience in one unified, *will she, won't she?*

Bethany's moment had come. She turned and walked away from Nick, conjuring disappointment and anxiety. But on the third step she turned back again to face Nick.

Even the barman was now transfixed and had halted pouring the wine for his customer.

She took a step forward. Forty eyes watched the way her waist moved; another forty were on her chest, imagining what was contained beneath the sequins, engrossed in their lustful reverie. Bethany held out her arm towards Nick. Her index finger emerged as she turned her palm upward. Slowly she curved it, hooking him in.

Nick eyed Bethany. Perhaps it had been her knickers he was wearing this morning. She was all right wasn't she? Quite the fox! He let the audience buy into the stand-off for a few seconds. Bethany's arm had now returned to her waist. With that Nick paced towards her. He'd take her; he'd show her what a stage kiss was all about!

Bethany put her arm up, taking the full impact of his

stride, with her hand on his chest. Nick was successfully disarmed. The look of raw and honest frustration was apparent on his face. Bethany's poker face was unchanged. She let her index finger once again take control, letting it slide up Nick's chest, running up over his shirt collar, tracing up the profile of his Adam's apple, over his chin and then letting it rest on his lips.

Eighty ladies hummed their approval, to see a man's earnest endeavor checked with one digit. Eighty men wanted to see Bethany's arm pushed aside. Forty ladies wanted to be Bethany, the other forty wanted to know what Nick would do.

Bethany took a step to her left, keeping Nick stationary with her finger. She stepped towards him and gently kissed him on his lips, beside her finger.

She turned around and bowed. The audience spontaneously applauded and those that could wolf-whistle did so.

Bethany turned to Nick, winked, and waved goodbye.

Nick let the applause die away. "Well, guys, that is how it is done! Come on, we have two tickets to be won. Who's next?"

The audience was noisy in their discussion.

"You do something!"

"No, you!"

"I thought she was going to kiss him!"

"She's a tease."

"He's a perv."

"Is this the show then?"

"She was gorgeous, wasn't she, that girl!?" Graham said to Craig. "What a holiday that would be, hey?" he winked. Susan and Melanie looked at each other in united condemnation.

"What about you then?" Graham was talking to Bert. Everyone turned to Bert and Tilly. "Have you got a sexy show for us?" Graham's voice broke into jeering laughter, hoping to enthuse the rest of the party.

Bert stood up.

"Ah, a volunteer," Nick was in, "or are you looking for the toilet? Is the prostate a little enlarged?" Tilly pulled at Bert's sleeve for him to sit down again. "The Gents are along the corridor." The audience chuckled with laughter. It was a welcome relief from the unease of thinking what they could do.

Bert hushed the audience by walking towards Nick. Walking as quickly as he could, he briefly turned to smile at Tilly. As he approached he gestured for the microphone. Nick complied.

"My wife and I would like to show you something."

Nick took back his microphone. "Well, guys, we do have a volunteer. A round of applause, please. And what is your name, Sir, and your good wife?" Nick was perplexed, for this was an unlikely volunteer. He didn't usually bother with the oldies as they had too much reserve. It was too hard to melt their frozen cage.

"My name is Bert, and I will be performing with my wife Tilly-Bu... er, Tilly."

"That's lovely, and is your wife on board this evening?" Bert looked confused. "You do have a wife, don't you?" The audience tittered.

"Yes, yes!" Bert was unaware of the mocking. "She will need a little encouragement. I wonder if you have some dance music you could play?"

"I love your style! You're going to woo your wife with a little music. What did you have in mind, a bit of Lady Gaga?"

Bert waited for the laughter to fade. "Do you have something for a foxtrot, or a quickstep?"

Nick looked to the sound desk. "What do we have guys, what can you do for us?" He put a finger to his ear. "Bert they don't have anything called that, but they do have 'La Cumparsita', which they assure me will put a smile on your face."

Sure enough Bert immediately smiled in response. "A tango, brilliant. It's been a while, mind, but we'll have a go, won't we, Tilly?"

Tilly had not yet stood up.

"I don't know, mate." Nick pretended to have a quiet talk with Bert. "I think you may be doing this little number on your own." The audience could not contain their mirth.

Bert went to the middle of the dance floor and held out his hands dramatically, as though he might be singing to the moon. The music started and he kicked out his left leg, angled his back and brought his arm down in a big swoop, which ended open-palmed and pointing at Tilly.

The audience looked on in dread, *is this poor man going to have to dance on his own?*

The violin continued its sultry tune. Bert coyly turned one hundred and eighty degrees. His back was straight and his arms were now folded. The snare gently began to tap out the beat. For four bars he continued to hold his pose. The audience began to talk amongst themselves, almost in sympathy to relieve Bert's embarrassment. As the clarinet released the main refrain, like champagne from a bottle, Bert turned just his head so that he was looking over his shoulder.

At that moment the audience noticed that a woman had appeared on the dance floor, as if from nowhere, holding herself like a statue and looking towards Bert. But as Bert's eyes fell upon her she looked away, and began a slow sweeping spiral across the dance floor, but not towards her husband.

Bert watched her continue to bisect the dance floor and then, in three graceful strides, glided to block her exit.

Tilly stopped, her face irritated at the intrusion. Not making eye contact, she looked around for a new path.

As she stepped diagonally, Bert held out his left arm, capturing her waist. With the other arm he pulled her towards him. Bert was now behind her, tracing her arm from her hand along to her elbow, lifting it until he felt her wrist. He whispered, "Give it all you've got, Tilly-Bum. Let's show these kids what sexy on the dance floor is all about!"

Tilly's back arched, the back of her head nestling on Bert's shoulder. The audience was mesmerised. Even Nick forgot his derision.

Bert's right leg came around Tilly's as he tapped out the syncopation, but Tilly kicked up her foot over Bert's and her heel turned away from him, leaving Bert's arms empty and his face forlorn. Tilly raised her chin, pouting her independence, and set off again. Bert seized her left arm and as he turned he pushed her around in a complete circle, leading her back to his front. "Promenade," he whispered. He stepped forward, enveloping her with his arms as each hand found hers. And then in one graceful movement, they both turned around, back-to-back, while not letting go of each other's hands.

Bert brought his arms down to finish with them around Tilly, bringing her tightly towards him. His right hand in the small of her back and his left hand holding hers far out to their side and up high.

Nick had forgotten to use his microphone. He was lost in the memory of seeing his own parents at a tea dance when he was a boy. His mother and father had gone religiously and taken him with them, hoping he'd learn. It was the highlight of his parents' week, the banter and the chit-chat. They seemed to know everyone. He was back there, watching from the sidelines the beauty they created.

How long had it been since he'd seen them, talked to them, emailed them? A pang of regret and the realisation that he'd lost contact with a couple of important people hit him. He struggled to refocus on his own performance.

Bert's hand wound around Tilly's waist and traced up her back, pulling her in so that their faces were inches apart.

"I need to sit down," Tilly whispered, "I do feel a little giddy." Bert kicked his toes up, back over and above her outstretched leg, and then finally back once more, this time leaning her slightly over as he held her around her waist.

"Ooh, that's enough, dear, come back!" Bert grimaced.

Tilly came forward and kicked the lower part of her right leg backwards and then forwards between Bert's lower legs. The audience followed them intently, silent in their captivation.

"Tilly, you still got it! Do the flick."

Tilly put her left hand on Bert's shoulder and pushed him back and around. As Tilly pretended to escape, Bert caught her hand and turned her back and around. Tilly's right hand clasped at the air in an attempt to break free. "You've got about fifteen seconds and I'm done!"

Bert ran his hand down Tilly's back as he held her cheek-to-cheek.

"OK, dear, do the 'Statue'."

Bert paced away from Tilly in two giant chasses,

ending in a dramatic flourish as he brought his arms up to the sky and then down. Tilly recovered quietly, impersonating the love-struck woman with her hands placed theatrically over her heart. Bert had danced to the chair that Nick had left behind. In one movement he swept the chair around him and then lightly brought it down, letting it glide over the floor, spinning as it went. The chair stopped inches away from Tilly. The audience spontaneously applauded. There were whistles and calls of "Bravo".

Tilly sat across the chair with her arm on its back. *Ooh, that felt good*, she thought. Now all she needed was a cup of tea.

Bert began his masterly glide around the dance floor, the intensity of his last conquest spurring him to reach new heights. He felt his dizziness come on. *Better make that the last twirl*, and with that he made a direct path for Tilly. As he approached her he came down to his knees and slid the last foot. Fifty years ago that would have been four.

He grabbed Tilly's hand and with his other he lightly cupped the back of her head as they made their mock kiss, with a full inch between their lips. The DJ had sensed the end and professionally killed the music. The audience erupted in adulation.

"I hope you haven't stretched those trousers," she giggled.

"You were amazing!"

"Come on, let's take a bow."

Bert offered his hand to help Tilly from the chair, and then they bowed to the audience.

Nick tapped the microphone. "Laydeez and gentlemen, give it up for Bert and Tilly." The small crowd managed to make a lot of noise, allowing them to take a second bow before they returned to their seats.

At that moment Bert felt something he hadn't had for quite a while. "Tilly dear, something's come up." He looked at her with confusion.

"Ah, that will be the purple pill!" She stood on her toes to speak into his ear, "It takes about thirty minutes to kick in completely. At least you managed to do your wonderful dancing first."

Graham was ready with his repartee. "Bert that was not bad for an old boy. Sexy, if not filthy!"

"Thank you, Grey-Ham. Yes, the crowd seemed to appreciate it." Bert grinned. "How about you, Melody, is that something you'd enjoy?"

Melanie smiled coyly. "I loved it, I've always wanted to dance like that. I keep on saying to Graham that we should start ballroom dance lessons, but he's just so busy."

Graham grabbed Melanie by the wrist. "OK, Mel, let's show them how it's done." Melanie resisted as she tried to stand her ground. She winced as she battled with Graham but he managed to pull her all the way to the middle of the dance floor. Melanie awkwardly stood next to Graham, looking up as if she were pleading for someone to come and save her. He put his hand around her waist and put his leg between hers, whilst his other hand kept hold of her wrist. Melanie recoiled and looked down at the floor. Her eyes darted to and fro as she appeared to be looking for a place to hide. Graham frowned, "Come on, we've got to win, do something sexy!" With that Graham swung her around and put his hands around her, his timing and agility somewhat out of practice. His hands found her boobs instead and his hips made an uncomfortable connection with her bottom. Graham seemed pumped up on a poisonous cocktail of adrenaline and wine. Melanie used Graham's shoulder to shroud her face. Graham's frown deepened. "Why aren't they clapping?" He put his arm out to the audience, open-palmed, "Come on guys, some applause."

Nick was ready. "Hey, guys, we have a new pretender, let's see what these two can do."

Tilly pulled Bert by his hand towards her ear. "Take me back to the cabin, darling."

Chapter Four

Tilly let Bert lead them into their cabin. As she closed the door behind them she studied his face. He took in the scene. Five candles were set out around the room, his silk robe had been laid on the bed and the radio was playing quietly. "Light the candles, I'm going to get changed." She stepped through into the toilet.

Bert felt the discomfort of the bulge in his trousers. "That purple pill," he called through the door, "was that Ve-a-gre?"

"Viagra, yes. The doctor said we need to be careful and monitor your heart, just make sure we don't get too carried away. There is a possibility your eyes may be sensitive to the light, it's a side effect. The candles will take care of that." He listened to the radio. It was playing a Cuban rumba from the forties. He let out his arms and spun around between their beds.

"Are you getting ready?"

Bert stopped and regarded the scene. "Just warming up dear." He sat on the bed and smiled. "I'd better put on the 'Do not disturb'."

"Yes. Now you've got it." As the rumba reached its climax, Bert turned again as if dancing with an imaginary partner towards the door. He deftly placed the sign in place whilst still keeping the pulse of the song. He let the beat set the pace for his hands and feet.

Tilly opened the toilet door and found Bert dancing. "Can I cut in, please?"

Tilly had changed into a black lace teddy.

"I haven't seen this for a while, dear. Didn't see you

pack it!"

"Now don't forget, if you feel your back going, we'll have to stop."

"Yes, dear." Bert pulled the black ribbon on Tilly's top.

"The doctor told me we need to counteract the purple pill with those beta blockers afterwards. But we have to be careful since it's your first time with Viagra so we don't know what will happen."

"I think we know what will happen, dear," Bert chuckled as he struggled to find the top of his zipper.

"Also, you can't take the Glyceryl for twelve hours as that will interfere with... Oh, I can't remember now, but anyway that's why you need a 'b' blocker."

"Right-o dear." He took the pill box from Tilly's hand and put it on the bedside table.

"Remember if you find your heart beating too fast, we probably just need to stop."

"And what happens if I find my heart isn't beating dear, shall I stop then too?"

"Bert, be good."

"Oh, I will be good." And with that Bert kissed Tilly in a way that he could not remember doing for quite some time."

"I feel like a bit of a virgin." Tilly giggled.

"I can remember you as a bit of a virgin, but I prefer it when you are a bit of a wench."

"Shut up and show me your magic trick."

Bert and Tilly lost themselves in a passion that was as rhythmic as their tango.

Somewhere on board the floating hotel, three thousand people were living out their lives to their hearts' content, attempting to find joy in whatever it was they were doing; some with more success than others. Many guests who had booked luxurious face massages were complaining about the value for money, and this was very much a hot topic of conversation, 'How much did you pay?' Others who had never had a cocktail before chose this week to try one for the first time, with one drink leading to another. Others developed complex strategies for ensuring that a certain sun lounger would be theirs for the next day, designing unwritten rules that others should observe.

Where there was an opportunity for laughter they found it. Others would always find a reason to complain and there was opportunity for that too.

"Tilly, are you, OK? You're looking strange."

"I'm fine... I'm feeling wonderful, dear – don't stop!"

"Right-o, Tilly-Snuggly-Bum."

"Oh, Bert, why on earth did we stop doing this?"

"Err, so that I could walk."

"Are you OK, darling?" Tilly saw Bert's pained expression had not subsided.

"It's my back, love. Could you just spray on some Deep Heat?"

Tilly curled her legs up and climbed out of the little roof structure Bert had made. Motionless, he resembled someone enacting a difficult yoga manoeuver.

"Don't move, darling, I know where it is."

"There's no worry about me moving. Can you be quick though?"

Tilly sprayed on the Deep Heat. The room quickly filled with the smell of vanilla, citrus and chili pepper.

"How's that, dear? Shall I get someone?"

"No! Just give me a minute."

"That purple pill still seems to be working," Tilly teased.

"Don't make me laugh!" With one hand Bert

managed to pick up the pillow and threw it at Tilly.

"Ooh, are we feeling better?"

He found the strength to sit up. "The great thing about a small room is that I don't have to chase you far."

"Catch me if you can."

*

Tilly and Bert sat at the breakfast table in a comfortable silence, occasionally turning to each other and smiling. They were the first to arrive on their table. They looked over the restaurant, taking in the extravagant decorations around the room, as well the meticulous presentation of the tables, each neatly set with white linen, polished cutlery and sparkling glasses. Smart waiting staff were kept busy, yet they remained efficient and polite. During the night the boat had transported them to Dominica. They were anchored on the sleepy side of a little port next to a steep-sided hill where wild banana, nutmeg and palm trees grew.

Tilly put her hand on Bert's. "This takes me back to our honeymoon."

"Do you think we've changed, dear?"

"Only on the outside."

Bert spotted Melanie approaching the table, her eyes fixed on the floor.

"Morning, Melody, how are you today?" Bert said as Tilly put their pill box back into her handbag. "Isn't it all wonderful? If you haven't already, you must have a quick walk on deck and take in the vista."

Melanie only managed half a smile. She sat down slowly. "I've been better."

"What's wrong, didn't you sleep well?" Tilly asked.

"We didn't win the competition." Melanie played

with the cutlery, "Graham likes to win." She looked up to see if her husband was nearby.

Tilly caught Bert's eye. "Oh, it's just a bit of silly fun."

Melanie still looked forlorn. Bert tried with a new tack. "I tell you what – why don't you have a walk with Tilly on deck after breakfast." He paused. "By the way, who did win?"

"He called out your names, but you weren't there, so this couple who re-enacted their marriage proposal won." Melanie looked up from stirring her coffee. "I loved your dancing, you two were wonderful."

"We could show you and Grey-Man a few moves if you like? There's a…"

"Morning!" Graham interrupted. "What happened to you two last night? You could have won the prize. Our table could have taken the victory!" He sat heavily in his chair and put his arm out straight towards the waiter. "Coffee here, please." He turned back to Bert for an answer.

"Oh, something came up," Bert smiled, "we had to get back to the cabin."

"That bloody Nick. It turns out that he did a nine month stint in Spain, working as an eighteen to thirty holiday rep."

"Eighteen to thirty? Is that a kind of period reenactment?" Bert asked.

"It's a bloody holiday company that specialises in organising events for people to have public and group sex parties." Bert looked vacant. "You know, a kind of hen and stag party entertainments planner, whose specialties include strip poker and sex games. All audience participation."

"Oh, I see – a bit like last night?"

"Yes, bloody vulgar!"

"Oh, I thought you were quite good, Grey-Ham, you seemed to be up for the show."

Graham started to turn red. "I didn't realise that he'd take us down that route. That's how they do it, you know. They work on slowly breaking down your inhibitions."

"Yes, I know! I can remember breaking down Tilly's inhibitions about sixty years ago!"

"Albert, be good!" Tilly slapped his thigh playfully.

"Well, I think it's outrageous! What on earth do P&O think they are doing bringing a man on here like that?" Graham frowned as he concentrated on stirring his coffee.

Tilly took out her pill box and cautiously broke the silence. "It was his idea for the game, but we all played it."

Bert had his say, "Yes, isn't that it, Grey-Ham? We all decide how we would play the game, or if to play at all."

"The point is that he wanted us to make a spectacle of ourselves, and bring every one down to his own base level."

"I don't know," it was Melanie's turn, "I thought his little sketch with Bethany was pretty harmless. It was sexy but he didn't even get a proper kiss. It was just a bit of fun. I think it's a bit like the game of life, there are many rules and everyone judges it differently."

"Ah well yes, the game of life, that's all subjective isn't it? No one can call that one," Graham continued, glad to steer the conversation away from last night.

Melanie was quickly in, "St Peter at his gate?"

"You don't believe that stuff anymore than I do. We all make up our own guidelines for that judgment"

"Number of friends?" Tilly offered.

"Money, car and house!" Graham raised his voice.

"Moments of laughter?" Bert suggested.

"Moments of passion?" Tilly giggled. Bert and Tilly looked at each other and Bert couldn't hide his elation.

Melanie noticed their exchange. "Oh my God," Melanie smiled at them, "You had an early night!" Bert and Tilly looked at the table cloth, smiling.

Graham, concentrating on catching the waiter's eye, was terser. "You should have stayed. You would have won!"

Tilly nodded, "It was getting a bit loutish, wasn't it? Not really my thing. Besides, when Bert dances like that it takes me back to our courting days."

"Everyone loved your tango. They were all talking about it after you left. We should learn to dance like that, shouldn't we, Graham?"

Graham remained silent, still hankering for another cup of coffee. He noticed Bert at the table, smiling with contentment. "You were very good," he said with little enthusiasm, "it's great that you're still dancing."

"Yes, good for them!" Melanie said, and then quietly she added, "At least they still can."

*

Melanie and Tilly leaned on the railing as they looked over the side of the ship. The shore was less than fifty yards away, and as they examined the rich vegetation, the sound of bird chatter and even the smell of bananas on the trees seemed to fill their senses. The early morning sun was warming them wonderfully.

"I really envy you, Tilly, in a nice way I mean."

"What my diabetes, arthritis and non-existent thyroid?"

Melanie studied the sun sparkling on the water. "For the way Bert looks at you. For the way he loves you."

"Ah love, well it's never constant, Melanie. It doesn't always feel like that. But yes, it's been more on than off, and I love him too!"

They let the stillness take over, allowing them to take in the Caribbean vista.

"So the pills you take," Melanie began, "they're not vitamins then?"

"Oh, no." Tilly chuckled. "Keep it under your hat, but those pills are keeping us alive. We really shouldn't be here, too much to go wrong. We're one of those reckless couples that gets taken off the ship in a helicopter with some life-threatening condition."

"Why did you come, then? Aren't you frightened?"

Tilly smiled as she formulated her response. "Yes, well, I guess it's Albert really, you could say he's terrified."

"Of dying?"

"No!" Tilly looked at Melanie, "of not living!"

Melanie raised an eyebrow and opened her mouth to speak, but instead she decided to let the silence continue. They watched the crew busy with their ropes and making ready the tenders. The small pilot boat leaving from the jetty. "Will you go on another cruise?"

"Possibly!" Tilly looked far into the jungle. "But I think we found what we were looking for. I don't think we need to be on a cruise ship to find that again."

Luke McEwen

Through the Eyes of Medusa

Prologue

When we think of Medusa we remember her rage, her ugliness and her wrath, and those eyes that turned men to stone. Yet in truth, if Greek mythology can have a truth, she had once been beautiful and pure. She had been the innocent victim of Poseidon's lust. Only by understanding the male-dominated society at the time can you understand why Poseidon could not be punished and why Medusa was mutilated and banished.

Chapter One

Simon threw his giant suitcase onto the bed. As it bounced up, his fingers flicked the catch and the lid flipped open. The silver photo frame that his mum had put in at the last second lay there on top. "It's a lovely frame, think of it as a moving in present," she'd said. He picked it up and saw himself staring back, with his blond unruly mop and that old silly tache, but there was Samantha too, looking away from the camera.

Mum just didn't get how he felt about Samantha, having finished that chapter in his life he really didn't need to be reminded of her. The way that she had said she wanted to break up was like being handed in at the dog rescue. "I got him for Christmas but I don't really want him anymore." She'd just been 'filling in time' before uni. He undid the back of the frame, took out the photo, folded her over and centred himself up. Simon spun around and let himself fall onto the bed, his suitcase bounced next to him.

He'd found his digs online, a bedroom in a shared house. When he'd arrived, the landlord explained that he was the only tenant for the time being, but that he was working on it. The house smelt of damp and it didn't quite resemble the modern spacious pictures he'd seen on the internet. It had made his arrival disappointing, all that on top of his tiring journey, Chester to Brighton on a train, what a day! It should have only been four hours but there were the inevitable delays and getting across London on the Tube with his life in bags had been a complete nightmare.

Dad had said he was running away, but he felt he was searching, and the inside of a shabby bedroom wasn't quite the answer he'd hoped for. With nursing you had to go where the job took you. Dad wanted him to be a mechanic at his garage and, yes, it was fun and interesting, but nothing compared to his passion for nursing. Being able to help people in their time of greatest need, in the most intimate of ways; that wasn't work, that was an honour.

He felt the suitcase watching him. He should unpack but instead he went to the window and drew back the curtains. Simon surveyed his view: the bus stop, the newsagents, the rows of identical buildings, the grey street, bare and treeless, and there almost opposite, the pub. It was a typical estate pub; an ugly modern building set in a car park with the addition of an abandoned car and dustbins overfull, all contained within a broken fence.

Even with the ceiling light on, the grey light of the afternoon made his room dark and the walls seemed too close together. A quick pint was in order; he'd check the pub out and unpack when he got back. After all, it was Saturday night. Without a second thought he pulled on his black top from the suitcase, brushed his teeth, ran his fingers through his hair and was gone.

*

Not being used to going into a pub where he was unknown and without friends, he pressed on the door with some trepidation. He just needed to find a friendly face for a quick chat, even if it was only with the barman. The landlord had said the pub was loud and busy, and as he entered he was not disappointed; it was just like home.

He surveyed the area. The bar swept around in a big horseshoe. There was a dartboard, a pool table, a TV showing football, and in the corner he saw large speakers and a drum set arranged in readiness. The chatter of the pub battled to be heard over an upbeat song.

He was conscious of being watched, *nothing out of the ordinary there,* he thought, *not for a pub on an estate.* A girl with long, dark hair sat at the bar, talking with the barman. Like a magnet, he was drawn to them.

"Hi, I heard you were a loud pub!" he said, immediately anxious that they might think his comment negative.

"Ah, just you wait," the barman replied, "it'll soon get louder. The Invitations are playing tonight. Have you heard of them?"

"No, I'm new here. Just arrived!" With that the girl looked up and smiled. Simon returned her smile. The girl continued to face the barman; her knees propped up on the bar stool, with her back straight.

The barman continued, "Great band if you're into rock."

"Yeah, I am. I used to play in a rock band myself," he quickly added, with his hand half raised, "many moons ago," so as not to appear too eager. Again the girl looked up and smiled. It was a warm and inviting expression. Not sexual, just friendly. Simon returned the smile but then looked away as he searched for something to say. He glanced at her again; he was worried that he might be staring for she was really gorgeous. She wore a black, see-through top over a skimpy, black blouse, with dark blue jeans and black boots.

"OK, don't worry," the barman laughed, "it's not an open mic session, you don't have to perform." Simon mirrored his laughter. The girl's head remained facing forward, yet her eyes briefly found his. Her lips parted, revealing dainty, white teeth, beautifully contrasted against her dark lipstick. One more time the flash of her eyes. Her mouth seemed to be holding back a little chuckle, as if she was waiting for him to speak. "What can I get you?" The barman raised his eyebrows.

"Oh, a pint please." He gestured to the pump in front of him.

The barman was still waiting and he looked across at the girl. Simon saw that she didn't have a drink.

"Can I get you one?" Simon said to the girl, feeling somewhat awkward.

"Ooh, thank you, that would be very acceptable."

Simon felt relief more than excitement and decided to formally introduce himself. "I'm Simon."

"Hi, I'm Kimberly."

She really is beautiful, Simon thought. He loved the way she spoke, confident and friendly, and with no sign of any accent.

"This your local, Kimberly?"

"This *is* my local and this is my barman, John." Simon wondered if she was implying that they were together. "So, what brings you to Brighton?"

"Work, I've got a new job. I've just arrived in town and I heard this was a really happening place."

The barman poured Kimberly a glass of white wine, without asking what she would like, and slid it in front of her.

"There you go, a new record. Seven minutes!" Kimberly announced to the barman. Simon couldn't work out what that meant.

"Thanks for the drink," Kimberly said as she slowly turned to face Simon. For the first time the right side of her face was visible to Simon. A red, ugly scar, two inches long, connected the outside corner of her eye with the centre of her cheek. Simon didn't flinch and kept on looking into her eyes. They were fixed and dark. He had a fleeting feeling that he caught a glimpse of rage in her eyes. As he continued to search for meaning in her expression her face softened, as though something had passed. "It's OK, you don't need to stay and talk to me if you don't want to." She turned back to the barman, showing her beauty again.

But he was already captivated. "I'd like to! Talk to you I mean. As I say I'm new in town. I don't really know anyone and you seem nice!" Inside he kicked himself, *no one says 'nice'!*

She turned back towards him, once again revealing the scar. "Don't waste your time if you just want to score a fantasy freak fuck." Her tone was not serious, just matter of fact.

It registered quickly that he was being tested, so he chose his words carefully. "There seems to be a lot more to you than just a scar…"

"Clever!" she said, "you can stay!" She looked at him, up and down, and for the first time took in his smart clothes, good posture and his manly good looks. "So what is it that brings you to the Blackhawk Estate? Not its fine restaurants and classy shopping." They both laughed.

"I'm a trainee nurse. I'm in my first year. I've been posted to Sussex County Hospital. It's only a ten minute bus ride from here."

"Ah, good for you. Shame you're not training to be a cosmetic surgeon." Simon felt that she was waiting for him to comment but he remained silent. "It's unusual for a man to be a nurse. Are you a caring man?" Her question seemed to be rhetorical. Again, Simon felt her observing him for a reaction, but he declined. "I actually think nursing is a very honourable vocation."

"Yes, a vocation! That means they get to pay me diddly-squit, next to nothing. I mustn't grumble, it pays the rent. What about you, what do you do?"

Kimberly didn't answer. "Your friend probably told you to come here for the music, they've got a live band every Tuesday and Saturday night. Tuesday is Jazz Night. Do you like jazz, Simon?"

Simon wondered if that was an invitation to invite her out. "Yeah, sometimes I listen to it. Not the traditional jazz stuff, I prefer it modern; although, a bit of fusion is great. How about you, are you here on a Tuesday night?"

Kimberly looked at him coyly, "I guess there's a first time for everything, perhaps it's best enjoyed with the right company." Her eyes were staring at his lips.

Simon finished his drink. "Like another?"

"Ooh, thank you, Simon, you are sweet." She slid her glass over to the barman. "You like talking to me, Simon?" she asked, raising one eyebrow.

"Yeah, you seem pretty special."

"Special? What special needs?" she teased.

"No!" he grinned. "Special, as in Mona Lisa's smile; the perfect sunrise; or the meal you once had and can't forget."

"Ooh, I like that kind of special!"

"Well, so do I."

She was nothing like Samantha, who had been so immature and just like Dad; she didn't really understand his passion for nursing. It felt so impermanent, so transient. What were those months all about? What did he have to show for all that he had done with and for her: the shopping, the hours practicing her interview technique, meeting her parents? Mum had almost laughed at him when he'd said that he was sad they'd broken up. "Don't fret, love, there'll be plenty more to come." But that wasn't him. He scorned men that put notches on bedposts; he didn't do casual.

Simon returned from his reverie. "Is this place your usual Saturday night routine?"

"Yup! Saturday nights are my only night out in the week. I get a free babysitter on a Saturday night. I can't afford to buy myself a drink, but I get a lot of drinks bought for me..." she paused, "...as long as I look west."

He ignored the reference to her scar and instead wanted confirmation. "You've got a child?"

"Amy. She's four. That put you off? Don't worry if it does, but you may as well tell me straight away and save us both the time." Simon was taken aback by her candidness; he didn't actually reply, but his mouth opened. "Well! Life is short so don't be so shocked. In life you need to say what you mean and then you don't disappoint and you don't get disappointed." As she grinned at him, Simon realised that he hadn't closed his mouth. "I tell you what, I'm going to the toilet. You can tell me what you think when I get back."

As Kimberley stood up and walked away from him, Simon took in her height and figure; both enhanced his desire for her. She was similar to Samantha: a cute little nose; graceful neck; and glossy, dark hair. Nevertheless, Kimberly was a woman, not a girl, a woman with a child. She seemed to know what she wanted and he liked the way she'd been clear with him. There was something about her that was definite and assured. Something that made him sit up straight and pay attention.

The barman leaned over. "Tread carefully there, mate, hey." His manner was not menacing; as so often happens when a man tries to warn another man off a woman he cares for. "I'm John, by the way. If you're new to the area you should know that the police always target this pub, on a Saturday, for drink drivers. Have you got accommodation sorted out? There are some people advertising on the noticeboard in the hallway."

"Oh, thanks for that, I've got a place sorted, but thanks anyway." He waited for John to finish serving a couple next to him. "So you've known Kim a long time then?"

"Oh yeah, Kim and I go back a long time, from school. Nothing romantic or anything. Yeah, she's lovely, she deserves some good luck."

"School days, hey, that's great." Simon's mind drifted back to his mates at home. Most of them he had met at school and it was weird to have left them all in Chester.

"At school she was one of the few that listened, worked hard and got her homework in on time. She wasn't a square or anything; she just wanted to better herself. She always planned to move on from Blackhawk. I had a bit of a crush on her to be honest, but I think she had her heart set on either Prince William or Jude Law!"

Kim returned from the toilet. "What are you saying, John, not giving away our secrets?"

"Not me, I'm too busy to have secrets."

John turned to serve another customer and Simon was pleased to have Kim all to himself.

"I'm still here!" Simon said, smiling, hoping that that would be enough of an explanation to answer her question.

"So you are!" As she sat down she used his knee to help her on to the stool. "So, tell me about Simon the nurse then. Now that you've given up trying to be a rock star, what are you into?"

"Ah well, there isn't much time for hobbies at the moment. I try and get in eight hours of study a week and there isn't much time left after work. But bikes are my thing. I have a Kawazaki z1000. It's in bits in my mum's garage right now, but I've had some good times on her. She looks great. You go to a meet and everyone is drooling over her. I get a load of offers to buy her, but I'm not interested, she keeps me happy."

"I love being on the back of a bike. I love all the leather and gear that goes with it!" Kimberly said, grinning.

"Well, I should have her fixed up in about a month. I could take you for a spin!" Simon was quite relaxed now; he hadn't even noticed that he'd asked to see Kimberly again.

"So, she just needs a bit of fixing, but essentially she's pretty special, is that right, Simon?" Kimberly teased.

"So, how did you get the scar?" Kimberley remained silent. "Bike accident?"

"If you want!" She looked at him, her eyes were on fire and her voice barely stifled her anger, or was it pure irritation? She turned away, as if hiding something. *Too personal, too soon*, Simon thought. "Sorry," she paused, looking genuinely annoyed with herself, "I just don't want to talk about it."

"No, that's OK, I shouldn't have asked." Simon wanted to bring the conversation back to something lighter. "So, do you like to ride bikes? I reckon you do." She nodded. "Do you ride pillion or have you been the driver?"

"I'm guessing pillion means passenger," she giggled, "no, I haven't got a licence or anything. I do fancy a go but it does look a little difficult....and dangerous! Are you a fast driver then, Simon? Do you break a few speed limits? Have you frightened a few of your girlfriends?"

"I don't know *any* biker who keeps to the limits!"

"Ooh, you missed the bit about the girlfriends!" She squeezed his forearm.

"I used to have a girl who liked the bike, but she moved away."

"Did you frighten her away?"

Simon laughed, "No, she moved on to university."

"Brighton!?"

"No, we're safe. So, when was your last boyfriend?"

Kimberly's eyes flashed, her lips pursed. "There have been men." She paused, making sure she had eye contact. "I'm no angel, Simon, but there's been no proper boyfriend." She hesitated. "Not since the accident."

Chapter Two

The bell for last orders rang. Kimberly and Simon looked at each other. They had spent the whole evening chatting.

"That came around quick!" Simon said, wanting her to acknowledge that they'd connected that evening. It had been a good night and Simon was bowled over that he met someone *so nice*. But now they only had a few minutes to decide on the next step.

"Are you coming back to mine?" she said, as she put her hand on his knee, sliding it towards his crotch.

"Oh, let's not rush things," Simon tried politely to hide his shock. "I really like you!"

"Bloody hell! You're serious, aren't you?" She removed her hand. "I offer you a shag and you're knocking me back!" His face dropped. An uneasy feeling of guilt and fear paralysed his lips. "I'm sorry, I didn't mean that." Kimberly calmed herself. "I just meant that I didn't want to be alone tonight." She looked frustrated. Frustrated that Simon wasn't saying anything. Frustrated that she hadn't said the right thing. "I don't meet men like you very often," she said, almost to herself. "You said you didn't mind about the scar."

Simon put his hand on her back and as Kimberly came forward his arm slid around her. "I just don't want to spoil a good thing!" he said, "you know how it goes if you rush it on the first night. It can really go wrong and then that's that." Simon sighed. "Oh bollocks, this is coming out all wrong. Of course I want to shag you, you're gorgeous! I just want to make sure we can do this next week."

Kimberly looked at Simon, "My God, you're the gorgeous one. Tell you what! Come back to mine and if I try to so much as kiss you, you can leave. How's that?" she grinned.

"Well OK," he said with mock submission, "how good's your coffee?"

The bar was at its loudest with some people shouting their farewells and others rushing to order one last drink. As they made their way to the door a group of people seemed to be watching them. As they approached their chatter cooled, and Simon thought he heard, "Another miserable fly in her sticky web."

Kim pulled on Simon's hand as she led him out.

*

"You can make coffee alright," Simon said, slurping from a big red mug. He looked around the kitchen, taking in the colourful assortment of hanging mugs and modern print roman blinds. On the fridge was a painting made from handprints, Amy's no doubt. The house was together, neat and clean. On the wall was a photo of Amy, her first day at playschool, perhaps. Golden ringlets sprung neatly from her head, like some blonde version of Shirley Temple. She looked happy, smiling confidently at the camera. Would Samantha have been a good mother? She might have left school, but she knew nothing about being an adult. Kimberly was sorted and responsible, she ran her own home.

"I like the way you've done your flat, have you been here long?"

"About four years now." She wiped down the worktop as Simon spied a single book in between a plant and the sugar pot, 'The Ladies Book of Etiquette'. Kimberly followed Simon's eyes.

"That was a present from my grandma."

"Was she trying to tell you something?" he teased.

"She was lovely. She lived pretty much her whole life in Norway. I only met her a few times, that I can remember anyway. She was so interesting, you know, sophisticated and well-read. Totally different to the rest of my family; she was tolerant, ...worldly; such a breath of fresh air. I didn't meet her until I was ten and I decided right off I wanted to be like her."

"Yeah, I know what you mean, sometimes you meet people and you know straight away, they've got it right, you can admire them, that you want to spend time with them. How come you saw her so little?"

"I never really got to find out why she'd gone abroad. She died shortly after she gave me the book."

"It's a bit weird though, isn't it? I see my nan every week, it's always been like that. She must have missed you all!"

Kimberly put her coffee mug on the worktop. "You know, I get the feeling you're going to talk to me all night. Would you mind..." she hesitated, "...and if we keep our clothes on and everything, can we get into bed now? And would you mind holding me?"

Simon was about to laugh at her forward suggestion, but there was something about Kimberly's look, which was so forlorn, that he was caught by her sadness. He couldn't put his finger on what it was. It was something overwhelming, and he was aware that he couldn't yet question her to find out what it could be.

"Where's the bedroom," he said, winking, "I must warn you that I do snore and I will need to borrow your toothbrush. I can't sleep without doing that!"

"Borrow my toothbrush! That's pretty bloody intimate, that's like kissing," she said laughing. She stroked his cheek and then ran her index finger over his mouth. "You could put your lips on mine, that isn't too bad is it." Simon looked concerned. "Blimey, you really are strong! I promise I'll keep my lips closed." Simon bent down and softly met her lips. For a first grade kiss it was long, but Kimberly kept her promise.

As they lay in bed Simon held Kimberly from behind as they talked a little. Soon Kimberly drifted off, moments later Simon followed.

*

"Coffee? Coffee, Simon?" she said, gently running her fingers through his hair. Teasing him slowly from his dreams. "How did you sleep?" Her hand explored the new stubble down the side of his face and brushed the hair from his eyes. "I slept like a baby." Simon's hand reached out to find her. "I don't think I've ever slept that deeply." Her finger ran over his chin and down over his Adam's apple, finding the hair on his chest. "And it wasn't the alcohol."

Simon forced one eye open to look at his watch, it was midday. They'd been sleeping for nearly eleven hours. "Wow, well I must have slept well. Hey, by the way, you're the one that snores!" She looked at him, her face apologetic and guilty. "No, no it was fine, it was actually very sweet." But he heard the worry in her silence. "Really!" he said softly, squeezing her hand on his chest, "I don't think I have every held someone for so long. We've skipped breakfast, let me cook you some lunch?"

"You're staying!?" Kimberly's voice failed to hide her surprise and then with further disbelief she asked, "Can you cook then?" With both of his eyes closed Simon enjoyed the last few seconds of being half asleep and half awake. The joy of having her there, watching over him. He pictured her face; he'd heard the surprise and delight framing her words.

"You know that meal I told you about, the one you can't forget? Well, my mum does it all the time. If we were back home we'd be getting on the bike right now to join them." He paused as he imagined them doing that. "But it doesn't matter, I got my mum to teach me the whole thing. I do the second best roast lunch in England!"

"A very talented man! So, you think I'm a girl that you could take home for Sunday lunch?"

He put his hand around the back of her neck, pulling her gently towards him. "No tongues, I haven't brushed my teeth."

But Kimberly had other plans. "Kiss me properly, I can't wait any longer."

Simon's reticence and reserve vanished as he let himself luxuriate in the kiss of someone that he found both beautiful and sexy. Her kiss seemed so much more absorbing than Samantha's.

Suddenly Kimberly pulled her head back. "I've got to get Amy!"

"Oh, OK!" He saw Kimberly look at the door, her lips tight. Simon tried to work out what that meant. "Would you like me to go?"

"I don't know." Kimberly's face looked even more anxious. "Amy hasn't seen me with a man before!" Quietly she thought it through. The silence continued until finally Simon offered what Kimberly was hoping for.

"I'd like to meet Amy, if you'd like me to. I know that's a big thing for Amy..." he paused, "...and for you. I guess we'll never know for sure until we start. It seems pretty good so far..." his face relaxed, "I don't need to change nappies or anything?"

"She's four!" Kimberly said, pushing a pillow onto his face.

"How about I go home, get changed, then come back and we'll all walk down the pier?"

"Wow! Yeah, I'd really like that." Her fear now completely dissolved.

As Kimberly rose from the bed her bare thigh was revealed; he saw a patch of short white lines but they were too uniform for stretch marks. He decided not to ask about them.

*

It had been a day of relaxation and fun. Simon had loved playing with Amy. She was the same age as his niece, who he was missing. The three of them had gelled together as though it had always been like that.

That evening Amy had been put to bed and they both sat on the sofa together. Simon had his left leg up on the cushion, while Kimberly sat between his legs; both faced the dark screen of the lifeless TV.

"It seems a little unreal," Simon started, "like, a bit of a dream!"

She pinched him playfully. "I'm real enough, I'm not sure about you!" she giggled.

"So why did you let me in?" Simon asked, "you haven't met a guy in four years and you pick me from a bar."

"I told you, I'm no saint, there have been men."

"Yes, but I'm the first to have met Amy!" Simon wore the badge with pride.

"It was what you said, 'I can see you're more than just your scar.' You didn't come out with a line and then..." she paused and then restarted her sentence, "you looked at my eyes and then my lips, but you never

57

ever once looked at my scar. You're the first person to have done that. Usually, I get left face, scar, a look at my tits and then some crap line, which means do you fancy a quickie. You'd be amazed. And then you get the 'look and run men'. Yeah, I've had a guy actually run away from me."

She moved herself away from Simon and sat on the other side of the sofa to face him. "You were so sweet, how you were nervous about being with me." She stretched out, leaned back and put her feet up on his lap. "And then this morning, when you were talking about your family and Sunday lunch, I guess that was a picture, such a beautiful picture."

"What about your family, is your mum local?"

"They're all dead!" she said abruptly, raising her voice.

Simon was quite taken aback. He'd put his foot in it again. "Oh!" He felt the same feeling he'd had at the pub and he knew that she wouldn't want to talk about it. "Was it the same car accident?" He had to ask.

"If you want!" She moved her feet off his lap.

Simon was quiet, noticing not for the first time and not for the last, when to ask and when not to ask a question of Kimberly.

*

A couple of months had passed and their relationship had grown strong. Simon spent so much time with Kimberly and Amy that the room he had arranged to live in became more of a storage and study area than a home. To an outsider the three of them looked very much like any other young family. He missed his friends in Chester. He missed the in-jokes and the nicknames. They'd called him 'Sandy' because of his hair, but that was one of the few things he was glad to have left behind.

He didn't like living on the estate, it wasn't the friendliest of places to be, far from it; many people were openly hostile. Once, whilst he was waiting for the bus, a car slowed down that had been full of people and as they passed him one had shouted, "Oi! Why don't you fuck off and take that bitch with you!" He'd been shocked. Every Sunday, knowing they'd be in, he would call his parents. He told them about the incident and they suggested moving out, so after that he didn't tell them anymore about the Blackhawk estate.

Nevertheless, working in the hospital was going well; it was everything that he had hoped it would be. The ward sister had taken a shine to him and Simon suspected it was because he was a man. Unfortunately, she did expect more from him, such as asking him to take more of the difficult shifts. She knew he had a girlfriend, but he couldn't help thinking she'd take advantage of him if she could get him alone. That was the problem with working with a lot of young nurses, they were always talking about sex and being a bloke often made him the centre of attention. He had complained about this to Kimberly, but she had not seen the funny side of it.

Simon's life was full. On top of all his studies and the busy hospital life, he enjoyed the family life he'd made with Kimberly and Amy. Kimberly was a loving and caring women, yet Simon often had to tread carefully around her. He initially put this down to the male-female divide, that was pretty much standard Chester culture, but he often felt there was something more to it than that. For a start, there was Kimberley's sleeping routine. Often she would talk in her sleep; once she had even woken herself up shouting. Simon couldn't make out the words but she was troubled, even frantic. He would hear things like, 'Get off' or 'Get out', and that was often accompanied by Kimberley's leg pushing against him, almost a kick, yet she would be fast asleep. When it was really bad he'd wake her up; although what was often more effective was to soothe her with soft words. Then when it was really bad there was the pillow routine: to prevent being woken up continuously he would stick a pillow between his legs and hers.

Simon noticed that people on the estate would watch them when they were out together. At first this seemed pretty natural, it's what would happen back at home. An estate was, after all, a neighbourhood of people. People have a natural curiosity about the people around them and in Chester he enjoyed this aspect of living in a community. But there was something slightly different about these people's interest. Their stares were more protracted than they should have been. There was no banter or exchange, be it an, "Afternoon," or a friendly, "hello." The Blackhawk estate was living up to its reputation.

Events slowly escalated. They were coming back from an evening out in Brighton. They felt the rain start to fall as they stepped off the bus and by the time they got to the door it was quite heavy. They both cursed as Simon fumbled with the key and as it finally slid into the lock a bottle was thrown at them, missing, but exploding against the wall, making a terrifying sound. Simon had hunched down automatically and looked behind and then up to Kim, who had stayed erect.

"Kim! Are you alright?"

"I'm fine, don't worry."

"The bastards could have killed us."

"If they wanted to have hit us they would of."

"What do you mean?"

"It's a warning, a scare."

"What like get out of town?"

She looked at him as though searching for another explanation, "Yeah."

The shattered glass that could so easily have hit them, now lay at their feet. Simon was more furious than scared and had his mobile out in seconds calling the police, but Kim had taken it from him and ended the call. "It'll make things ten times worse, it's how it goes around here, plus there's nothing the police can or will do."

"How can you be so calm?"

He had taken a week to find his composure, warily opening the front door to the silent war zone, and just as he was starting to calm down another example of Blackhawk hospitality emerged.

Simon had not given up trying to make a connection with the people around him, they were just normal people after all, surely after all these months they'd warm up a bit! As he walked to the newsagents for milk he passed a woman that he often saw and decided to try a cheerful, "Good morning!"

The women scowled and put her head down to pass by, but she called back at him, "You're with that slag!" Her face was screwed up. "She hasn't cheated on you yet then?!" Simon spent the next hour perplexed and shocked, almost not wanting to go to work. For the rest of his shift he mulled the incident over.

Work turned out to be, in fact, a great distraction from the stresses of the estate. On the following day, returning from work, Simon practically skipped off the bus. The sun felt lovely on his face and it had been a good day; he'd got the questions right from his mentor,

Miss Harton. She had asked about the correct procedure for changing a catheter and he'd got it right straight off; then he'd been allowed to inject a patient with insulin. But when he arrived home he was completely shocked by the sight before him. 'Slut' had been written in large letters across their white UPVC door. He stared in disbelief and the joy of the day dissolved in an instant. As he examined the writing he could see it had been smeared on. At first he thought it was mud, held in someone's hand, but his nose told him it was excrement. The door opened and Kimberly stood before him, with her hands in yellow gloves, holding the kitchen bowl filled with suds and her face full of shame.

"It's just a warning, is it?"

"It comes off easily."

"Does it? Maybe off the door it does, but you watch it linger under your skin. It'll break you, Kim!" She busied herself with the door. "What are we doing here?"

*

The next day, on the same journey to the bus stop, he recognised a man in the street that had been staring at him over the last few weeks. Simon had decided that enough was enough and it was time to find out exactly what was going. He approached the man, who seemed to be in his mid-forties. Initially he just kept his head down, trying to avoid any contact. But Simon was determined to have an answer; no matter how embarrassing it might be, or the likelihood that yesterday's outburst might be repeated as a consequence.

"Excuse me, please, sorry to trouble you. Do you know Kim?" The man was, as expected, reticent to reply and he looked awkward. "Who are you, an old boyfriend?" The man looked as though he was going to completely ignore Simon and pass by. "I don't want any trouble, I just want to know." Simon couldn't hide his frustration. "You don't know Kim, then?"

Finally he stopped. "I'm the dead father." He took a step closer to Simon. "I live with the dead mother and her dead sister." His manner was flat, neither sad nor angry. He looked to his feet as though he was trying to work out what to say. "Is she OK, is Kim alright?" His expression was unfolding with intensity.

"Yes!" he said defensively. "What happened, why aren't you talking to your daughter?"

"She hasn't told you?" The father looked up to Simon for the first time. "She told you we all died, I expect?" His face was now twisted. Simon nodded, anxious of what he was going to hear next. "Kim was found with my brother, having sex in his bed."

Simon was speechless.

"It was my sister-in-law that found them, you know, his wife; she's a hard lady, right?" His voice trailed off. "Anyway, she didn't control her temper. Do you get it...?" He paused. "Kim won't talk to me and the family won't have her name mentioned." He looked at Simon for comprehension. "I'd better go, they won't want me talking to you." He waited for Simon to say something, but Simon was trying to make sense of what he'd heard. "Goodbye," he finally said. Simon didn't respond and the man began to walk away. However, his pace slowed, he stopped and turned. "She just needs to show them that she regrets doing it. She should never have gone to the police, we sort things out amongst ourselves around here."

"OK, but you haven't sorted it out. Why haven't you sorted it out with Kim?" The father looked uninterested. "Anyway, I'm sure if she went to the police she had good reason."

The father's eyes became colder. "You know this probably isn't a safe town for you, especially if you're out with Kim at night. Make sure your doors are locked."

"What?"

"She thinks she's too good for us, that's her problem."

"From what I've seen she's the only one of you lot with any manners." Simon could feel his blood boil. "What kind of father talks about his daughter like that?"

The man launched himself at Simon. He grabbed Simon's arm and twisted it behind his back, pushing him up against the wall; Simon's face was hard against the brickwork. "Look, you little upstart, you fucking do-good nurse. Your slag of a girlfriend is a sex maniac, just like her slut of a grandmother." Simon smelt Kim's father's hot breath as he spat the words in his face. "Now just piss off to that little hole of yours and keep yourselves to yourselves. No one wants to see you around." He jabbed him in the ribs. "Do you get it?" He jabbed him again.

"Yeah, yeah, I get it."

With that the man slowly walked away.

*

Simon spent the day at the hospital piecing together the conversation and the events of the last few weeks. He asked for some codeine to kill the pain in his arm and ribs, but the busy shift was not enough to distract him from the insidious puzzle that appeared to threaten the core of his happiness. He thought about calling his parents but they wouldn't understand, they hadn't even met Kim and Amy. Why hadn't Kim opened up to him, did she not trust him? What was it with Kim's family, how did they know he was a nurse and what kind of people behaved like that? Why didn't Kim want to go to the police? Why did she act like nothing was wrong, like she could live with it?

On his return he hesitated at the front door as he struggled to meter his racing heart. Slowly he opened the door and found Kim in the kitchen chopping vegetables. He stared at her for a moment, who was she? Simon continued to watch as he remembered the father's words until finally she looked up.

"You alright, Simon?"

"Yeah, fine. You OK?"

"Yeah, not bad."

He'd heard the hollowness of his own voice and Kim had heard it too.

*

They sat on the sofa with the TV on quietly, Kim resting her head against Simon's shoulder. Simon was still recovering; his ribs were badly bruised. He patiently waited for an opportunity to start his inquiry. It actually had been a hard day at work too; his mental exhaustion made the task of comprehending the morning's events and formulating the right questions taxing. It all sounded so unbelievable and now his thoughts were a convoluted mess. Finally, in desperation, he gave up and just blurted out what he needed to know. "Have all your family gone? They've all died?"

She sat up, her back rigid, but she continued to look at the TV. "Every single one." Her eyes were severe and unyielding, her lips rutted in their closure. Then she turned to Simon, her eyes black and unfocused, "All of them!"

"Is that like, talk to the hand coz the face ain't listening? Kim, are you going to talk to me?" She stood up. "We should talk!" He stood up to stop her leaving.

"Don't!" Her face threatened him. "Don't, Simon!"

He put his hand out to touch her back but she shielded herself, lifting her arm between them, her hands now fists. He searched her face for an opening but her hardness was a shell, unwilling to shatter. "Sorry! I'm sorry, Kimberly." Once more he tried to put an arm around her, but her arm stayed upright with her hand against his chest. "Forget I said anything." He held her uncomfortably.

"Ask me no questions and I'll tell you no lies," was all she could mumble. Her breath was heavy. Simon could feel her heart pounding. Finally she let her arm drop from between them and he held her fully.

*

Simon arrived at the pub as it was opening. The morning light was failing to lift his spirits as he watched John unbolt the door. He'd awoken from an exhausting night of broken sleep. He remembered first reading the clock at three a.m. He'd tried hard to switch off from his thoughts; he needed sleep for his long shift. For hours he had asked himself the same questions but there didn't seem to be any answers. What couldn't Kimberly tell him? He was resolved to find an answer and had decided that the barman was the best source available.

"Hey, John."

"Oh hi, Simon! A bit early for you!" John dropped his grin when he saw Simon's face. "What's up, is Kim alright?"

"I met Kim's dead father." Simon just wanted answers.

"Oh! I'm not sure it's my place to say anything."

"I really need to know, John! She's really important to me. Surely me knowing will bring Kim and me closer. I'm not prying for the sake of it!"

John led the way into the bar, grateful that there was no one else around. "If you let on I told you, Kim won't speak to me again," he picked up a glass and started to dry it, "and she'll feel really let down." He paused and maintained his eye contact, letting his expression underline his warning. He took a deep breath. "Kim was raped by her uncle. She was sixteen, you know, still a virgin, but the family says that she's to blame. That she wanted it, that she'd always flirted with him." John looked around, checking the bar was empty. "The one that really goes on about it is the uncle's wife. She's the one that cut Kimberly's face."

"What?"

"It all happened at the uncle's house. They were having a family party. There was a lot of booze and he pushed Kim into his bedroom and forced himself on her. What's weird is that he's the family favourite. You know, the one that makes everyone laugh. He *is* the Blackhawk social committee, always raising money for charity. You'd like him if you met him. If you didn't know..." John paused, placing the glass on the shelf, "...the uncle though, it turns out, is a bit of a dark horse; that came out a couple of years ago. The guy is just a womaniser! The big thing for her is that she didn't fight her uncle off. She didn't struggle. No one believed her when she said she was raped. The whole family piled into the room and just thought they were having sex. She told me, after she'd had a few, that she never put up a fight because she loved her uncle, you know, like family, not in a romantic way. She was dazed when he went for her. She didn't know what to do and didn't want to hit him or anything. She was a little naïve then, she just didn't have the armour she has now." John raised an eyebrow. "It just wouldn't happen now, she's learned a lot over the last four years; she's not the same women at all."

Simon was stunned, not merely by the fact that Kimberly had been raped but by the inconsistency between John's account and the father's account of what had happened. "So, the family not talking to her, that all comes from the uncle, does it?" Simon asked.

"No, it was the wife, she was furious with Kim for going to the police; his mayor of Blackhawk reputation was under threat. That was a mini saga in itself. If you ask me though, her mother and aunt have always been jealous of her, of her good looks, her intelligence. They'd always give her a hard time, you know 'butt of the joke', give her too many chores, that kind of thing. Kim said she never felt like she ever really fitted in.

When the aunt found them she didn't shout or scream, she just went to the kitchen, grabbed a knife and stuck it in Kim's face, while he was still on top of her."

"Bloody hell!"

"The uncle didn't even know they'd been found 'til he heard Kim scream and saw all the blood."

Simon's jaw dropped in disbelief and his heart was now racing. "Did she…. What did Kim…"

"Kim came running around to mine. She was all covered in blood. I got a taxi and we were at the hospital in less than ten minutes, but being a Saturday night, it was busy. They couldn't see her for three hours. It turned out that she'd used a dirty knife and the cut couldn't be sewn up straight away. Then, with it being so late, they had to wait for a doctor to come in the morning. That's why the scar's so messy."

"Did you call the police?"

"Not on the night, Kim didn't want that, she was in a right old state and I realise that I should've persuaded her, but she was just so.... Well I'd never seen her so shaken up." John's voice became clogged.

"I'm sorry, John, I didn't mean to..."

"The thing with Kim is that she was different right from the start; she even spoke different from the rest of the family. Didn't like swearing, used to tell her parents off if they did. You know she tried to go to Sunday school, we must have been ten, but her dad actually wouldn't let her, he said it was a waste of time. Before it all happened she was going to go to university. She used to read everything and then after the.... the rape, she just stopped. You'll never see her with a book now.

Simon's head was swamped. "Thanks, John, I better go."

"You won't...."

"Don't worry, I won't say I've spoken to you." Simon paused at the door. "I knew there was something but I never would have guessed any of that. You've been a real mate to Kim. Thank God she had you around."

Chapter Three

Simon arrived back at the flat where he found Kimberly in the bedroom changing their sheets. He felt strangely guilty that he had been talking about her behind her back. "Hi, are you alright? How was your day?" Kimberley turned and held her lips up for a kiss.

"I'm alright thanks, but Amy's had a funny day." Simon held her around the waist as he kissed her. "Amy's been to school and they've been doing a school project on family. She's realised that we don't have any!"

Simon looked at Kimberley, wondering at what level she denied their existence. Was the lie so fully accepted that she believed it herself or was it just a complete mask. Perhaps it was somewhere in between? Would Kimberly even allow herself to think of them?

"What did you say to Amy, did you tell her about the accident?" Simon asked quietly. Simon watched Kimberly look up as if to judge his face. Did she know he was testing her?

"I think that it's too soon, she's so young. What's the point in her feeling that she's lost them if she never even had them!"

"What was it like being with your family, before the accident?" Simon felt a pang of anxiety. He'd phrased the question really weirdly but he just wanted to get her talking. He felt her look at him blankly, or was it suspicion? The silence became awkward. How far could he push her? "I love you, Kimberly." There was no romance in his voice and his expression was solemn. This was serious; he couldn't bear to see her so trapped.

"And I love you too," she said, mirroring his tone, "but I wonder if you would love me if you *really* knew me?"

"Well, that's what I'd like to find out." Simon's voice was a little louder.

"It's been a long day, Simon. I really just need to relax."

"But Kim…."

"Look, Simon, not everyone had a rosy cottage upbringing. If you can't respect my privacy, which is a sign of respect after all, …..that's not too much to ask, is it? Perhaps you should leave!" Simon couldn't help but give her a severe look, he picked up his keys and then his phone. "What, you're walking out on me just like that?" She stood in front of him, blocking his exit. "I'm sorry. It came out wrong." Her intonation did not match the apology.

Simon saw that she wasn't ready to talk. His direct approach wasn't working. "Sorry, Kim, I didn't mean to….. Look, you go put your feet up and play with Amy. I'm going to make you a bucketful of tea." He grabbed her hands, and kissed her gently on her forehead.

"A mug will do," she said, trying to find her softness. The relief that she'd been excused was visible on her face.

*

Simon started the nightly routine. "When this is over, Amy, we'll get you into bed."

"Aww, Simon."

"You've still got ten minutes. If you want, we can turn the TV off and play a little game."

But the lure of the TV was too much so Simon tidied up Amy's toys as she watched. Once face-time, teeth-time and pyjama-time were over, Simon read to Amy as she arranged her dolls on the windowsill.

"...and they all lived happily ever after. Right you, into bed then."

"Will you say the Amy poem?"

"Alright then...

Amy's locks are cute and curly.
Not like Simon who can be surly
No monsters in my bed
No monsters in my head
Just kisses and hugs
No more bed bugs
For Amy isn't gonna wake up early!"

Kimberly added from the door, "And if you do wake up early, no getting out of bed!"

"It's important to sleep, it'll make you clever like your mum."

"And beautiful like Mum."

Amy received her kisses and they left her room; Simon gently pulled the door to.

"Where are you going for your staff party then, tomorrow isn't it?" Kim walked ahead of Simon to the kitchen.

"Oh yeah, I'd almost forgotten."

"A night out with a load of young nurses, yes, how could you forget?"

"It's work, they just think of me as one of the girls."

"Yeah, right! You've told me what a load of nurses are like on a night out."

Simon sat down and pulled Kimberley onto his lap. "It's just work, but yeah, it's fun."

"So did you want to borrow a dress, you being one of the girls and all that?" Kimberley briefly stood, turned round to face him and then sat down straddling his knees. "Something low-cut perhaps? Does my man have a bit of cleavage envy?" Her hand pinched his nipple.

"Oi!"

"I bet it's fun being centre of attention with all those nurses spoiling you. Do they all want to practise their mouth-to-mouth resuscitation on you?"

"I'll be back by eleven! And no, they don't spoil me, more likely I'll be the butt of all their teasing. And if there's a practical joke going around, guess who'll get it?"

*

Later that evening, when Amy was in bed, Simon was still anxious that Kimberly was still upset. They were settled in front of the TV, watching their favourite talk show.

"You OK, Kim, are you still worried about Amy?" he asked, trying to build back the rapport.

"I'm quite acceptable, thank you." Kim answered in her sweet way. "Hey, I didn't tell you about the good stuff! There's a place at Amy's nursery for an assistant and they've asked me to apply. It's not bad money and you can take some training and get a certificate."

"That's excellent!"

"See, it's not just you that's clever."

"Good for you!" Simon was relieved. He knew it would be a great opportunity for Kimberly; it really was just what she needed. "When do you start?"

"If I get it then I could start straight away, next Tuesday!"

"Tuesday? Tuesday's your birthday! I guess that doesn't matter. We can celebrate on the Sunday instead. Hey, I'm off too. What do you fancy doing?"

"Fly me to Paris please," Kimberly giggled, "a champagne breakfast at the Eiffel Tower. You can take me to see that picture you were telling me about, the perfect Mona Lisa."

"Yeah right, shall we take the private jet?"

"Oh yes, better get James to get some good grub on board. We don't want any M&S ready meals!" she laughed.

"Who's James?" he demanded with a smile.

"Ooh, are we jealous?" James is the pilot, like James the chauffeur, you know, keep up!"

"Well, I'll tell James to pack the Bolly and the Spam, and I'll fry you up some fritters."

"Spam fritters and champagne, you really know how to spoil a girl!"

"Oh no! I've just realised the private jet is in for its M.O.T at the weekend. How about I take you to another city?" Kim looked up intrigued. "How about the three of us go up to London for a day out?"

"Yeah, cool!" She looked cheerful. "Paris does get a bit chilly this time of year."

*

The day had begun well. Simon had delivered perfectly prepared bacon butties to Kimberly in bed and she had declared it the best start to a birthday, "Ever, ever, ever!" Amy was in good spirits and she had been entertained on the train with a pen and paper, doing some doodling. They had arrived at Victoria station for their big day out in the city.

There wasn't much of a plan but when they arrived, and found wonderful sunshine, they decided to walk from the station to Buckingham Palace. Simon wanted to show Amy the Changing of the Guard ceremony. Luckily they had arrived just in time to see the mounted Life Guards on their horses parading down St James.

"OK, birthday girl, what do you want to do now?"

"Ooh," Kimberly put a finger to her cheek. "I know. If we can't see the Mona Lisa in Paris, let's see some pictures here!"

"No problem!" Simon said confidently. He took out his mobile and made a quick internet search that mapped out four galleries. "There's a big one in Trafalgar Square! Come on, you lot, it's only five minutes from here."

*

The building had transformed Amy. The huge canvases in the dark, long rooms had made her unusually subdued.

"It's like being in a library, isn't it, Amy?" Simon tried to make her feel more relaxed.

"Do we have to learn stuff?" she asked with a frown.

"No, we've just come to look at all these pictures."

"Well, can we talk? You can't talk in a library."

"We can talk. You're supposed to talk. Talk about the pictures, whether you like them. What story they tell."

"Well, what's this one about?" Amy said, pointing to a large oil painting. "Why are those people all grey?"

Simon looked and was shocked at the scene in the picture. He'd never seen it before but recognised the story from a Greek fable. It was an ugly picture. If pictures could have certificates this would have a

75

certificate 18. It wasn't suitable for Amy and he walked on.

"What is it Simon? What's going on?" Amy insisted.

"It's just a story; a story about Medusa. Her head is covered in snakes. If you look at her face, she'll turn you to stone."

"That's horrible!" Amy let go of Simon's hand and walked on to the next picture.

Simon was going to follow but was aware that Kimberly was looking intently at the picture.

"That's quite a gift," Kimberly said quietly, "just think, no need for a trial, just the judgment. Their death is instant. No agony, no screaming. In an instant they are no more. You don't have to hear the recriminations." From the corner of his eye he saw that the picture had absorbed Kimberly. He concealed his anxiety as he observed her. Was she imagining wielding the monster's power?

"Yes, that's quite a gift. Sort out all kinds of problems, that." Simon found his mouth was dry and he felt the urge to catch up with Amy. In that moment he became more determined to unlock Kimberly from her prison and by the end of the afternoon he had formulated his plan.

*

By early evening they had returned home. Simon cooked his signature dish of roast lamb, with all the trimmings, to mark Kimberly's birthday. He'd opened a bottle of wine as part of the celebration and he made sure that he had her glass topped up throughout the meal. Amy had joined them for the roast, but afterwards they put her to bed. She was quite tired from their long day out.

"Did you enjoy your day?" Simon asked as he poured Kimberly another glass of wine.

"Well it wasn't Paris, but it was wonderful." Kimberly hadn't quite pronounced wonderful correctly; the wine had had its effect. Simon decided she was drunk. Drunk enough for what he needed.

"You were quite taken with that Medusa painting. I wonder if it was really a metaphor?" Simon had tried to be casual but knew his opening had been clumsy.

"A what-a-four?" Kimberly giggled.

"Go on, you loved that picture. The power she had, damning those people with just a look. I wonder what they'd done to deserve that?"

"Probably been disloyal bastards," she said, quite animated, "probably completely pissed her off. They had it coming!" She slapped him playfully on the knee.

"What about you, who's pissed you off that much?" Quite sober, he felt the pang of anxiety again. Was that a bit close to the mark, would she notice?

"Oh, I've had a few moments in my life, moments when people have completely deserted me. People, who should really be with you through thick and thin, just turn into some rubbish traitors. Walk past you in the street as though you weren't there, as though they didn't know you from Adam." Kimberly's voice was now harder and louder. "I tried all sorts, tried smiling right at them, but they've already seen you and they just don't look up. I sent Christmas cards, emails, messages on the answerphone saying, 'let's get together!'" She mocked her own voice by sounding overly sweet. "Stupid foolish girl!" Then she quietened down, "They think I'm a monster. No Christmas cards, no birthday cards. What's bizarre is that one day they were all there and one day they weren't." Her voice became only just audible, "Yeah, I'd fallen out pretty badly with some of them before, but not with all of them. Just little tiffs. People come around eventually, but not this time." She took a mouthful of wine, "It was a question of either believing in their lies or just believing they had died. Believing they were all dead, that was so much easier. I can't work out what I did to be such a monster. I loved my mum and my dad. I thought that they loved me, but their love was a sham, it was nothing!"

Kimberly looked right at Simon; her eyes were dark, her expression cold and her scar red. "I got used up and dealt a death blow in one crazy moment." Simon didn't dare look at Kimberly, so as not to distract her. The poison was coming out and he wanted it all out. Kimberly started to cry. He had put his arms around her when she had begun to talk and now he could feel her sobbing. Her whole body convulsed. And then it happened, like a dam bursting, her sobs turned to shrieks as her tears flowed freely and uncontrollably. Simon was worried that he wouldn't be able to stop what he had started. Had he been right to even unlock this pain? Would she blame him for the hurt she was feeling?

"The bastards! The fucking bastards!" Kimberly thumped the sofa. The force knocked the TV remote off and it clanged on the floor. He couldn't bring himself to contain her anguish, he felt so unqualified to begin to respond to it. He thought of things to say but they all seemed glib and formulated. This was a rare opportunity and if he could get her to tell him everything then hopefully he could help her deal with it.

Very quietly Simon probed, "They hurt you?"

"He fucking raped me!" she shouted. She roughly grabbed Simon's chin and pulled it around for his eyes to meet hers. With the other hand she grabbed his shirt and pulled him to her. "He raped me and then the whole lot of them came into the room, got around and jeered and poked at me, like I was some kind of animal. Calling me a whore! I couldn't cover my boobs. They kept on pulling my arms away, as if I'd chosen to be naked! My aunt was trying to stick the knife in again. Only a few were trying to hold her back. Animals! Savages!"

Simon saw her courage. She was throwing off the badge of lies they had tried to make her wear. "What else, Kim? What did they do?"

Through her tears she whimpered, "They told the police that I'd slept with my uncle, that I slept around, that I was only angry because I'd been caught!" Kimberly was even quieter now, her sobbing suddenly over. "He raped me, she stuck me with a knife and then the family threw me out." She sniffed in her tears. "It was all over in flash, my life ended in a moment!" She rested her head on Simon's shoulder. "I had no home, I had no money, no one would talk to me. The police treated me like a thing. Like a slut." She finished her wine. "I went to this home, there were a load of druggies, prostitutes, women with babies, kids who'd had kids, they were my new family," she turned her head to face Simon, "and I tell you what, they didn't have a lot but they had tenfold the heart my family had."

*

They lay there for over an hour while Kimberly recovered. Simon was quietly elated, for it seemed that his love could be complete now. He felt that he could build on the ruins, now that he knew their foundations.

Kimberly laid curled up on the sofa, her head on Simon's lap, almost asleep and her energy drained. "Shall we go to bed, you must be exhausted?"

"They don't even want to meet Amy! How could a father be so cold!?" Her voice became more urgent, "Simon, there is something you should know. When he touched me I was shocked, I didn't fight him off. I told him 'no', 'stop it', 'I don't want it', but I didn't actually hit him. They said I must have wanted it otherwise I would have fought." Simon was silent; stunned by the realisation that somehow she was accepting some blame. "Over the years I've been looking back, trying to work out what I should have done. He was my uncle and I loved him. He was a great guy, so funny and I was his favourite. He called me his little Princess."

"It must have been awful."

"I was totally on my own. There was absolutely no one in the world that wanted to be with me. I felt so worthless; it was like I was invisible. I can still see his face now, when he was on top of me... his smile. You know for years I thought he was smiling with pleasure, you know, the sex. Then I realised the smile was all about his power, not so much him taking away my innocence, but about him rubbishing it, destroying it, making me soiled, sordid, like the rest of them. I hadn't been with a man before, I was proud of that, I think that must have annoyed a lot of them. Perhaps it annoyed him too?

I was going to end it, you know, lights out forever, but then I found out that I had Amy; she was tiny, inside me, I felt her and I couldn't let her down. I remember I cried, I couldn't stop crying. I tried calling up one of those helplines but the words never came out. I just cried down the phone. They kept on saying, 'We're here for you', but they weren't, no one was. All I had was the cutting, but then that hurt too much. I took to the craft knife in the end. It was uncontrollable, I terrified myself. I couldn't stop it and I didn't know if one day I'd just cut too deep.

I'd wake up and hate the fact I was still here, that I hadn't died in the night. I'd spend whole weeks on my own. For two months the only people I saw were the midwife and the social worker, and they didn't really want to stick around. It was the feeling that I was nothing, not a person, just a thing, forgotten. Only six month before I'd had everything: family, friends, a place where I belonged. There wasn't one person in this whole world that cared if I was alive or not. Some days it comes back, it comes back really strong, like people are looking at me, talking about me, like everything I do is wrong."

Simon felt her torture, the years of pain she had given herself. "No, Kim, you did nothing wrong. You did your best." He kept his arms tightly around her. "It starts here, Kim, right now!" He gently moved his hand into hers. "I want you to forget about taking any blame. How can it be your fault? You just didn't know how to handle him; there is nothing more to it than that. I can't believe the police, the system, let you down so badly. Come on, let's get you into bed, you must be exhausted."

"I've had enough!" Kimberley sat up. "I really have had it, no more! Enough of the lies, their turning it all around. It's all crap. All of it's just shit. They're a load of scum. I wish they would all just die, right now! But what can I do, the police just think I'm a troublemaker." She cradled her head between her knees. "This pain just won't leave, it goes around and around and whichever way, I just can't work it out. Sometimes I wake up and it feels like I'm empty and nothing will fill it. If you're at work and Amy's at playschool, I can't stand being at home. It happened the other day, I thought I'd paint the kitchen. I didn't last more than half an hour before I went and collected Amy."

Simon held Kimberley whilst she calmed down and he finally persuaded her to go to bed. She was out within moments. As he fell asleep he felt grateful. Grateful he was no longer on the outside. Instinctively he knew that she would keep on torturing herself, and that he didn't know how to explain to her that she shouldn't, but they'd made a start.

*

Simon had slept deeply and awoke with the same sense of peace and relief that he had fallen asleep with. The room was gently lit by the glow of dawn and Kimberly was still fast asleep. He felt different: lighter and stronger. Last night was the dam that burst, and now it was as if he were downstream, enjoying all the freshness of a newly washed clean world.

He made them both a cup of coffee and brought them back to bed. Sitting up, he waited for Kimberly to come around. He couldn't help but stroke her hair, even though he knew he might wake her. He wanted more of the connection they'd made last night, with him on the inside, as her confidant.

How funny that he'd known her for so long, but had only just begun to understand her. If he hadn't of pushed for the truth, how much longer would he have waited?

"What are you thinking?" Kimberly asked quietly.

"Coffee, Kim." He passed her the mug.

"Go on, tell me, what are you thinking?" she persisted.

"That I've only just got to know a big part of you." Kim's face changed as she felt her guilt. "No, I mean you never hid from me that there was something you didn't want to talk about. You made that clear, but I just didn't realise it was so big."

"Is it such a big thing?"

"Yes, Kim, it is! I think your family are all dead and then it turns out they're walking around us like some kind of weird zombie film!" Simon wanted to keep the mood light, he didn't want another big session. Kimberly needed to recover. As much as he wanted to help, in the end it would be Kim that healed herself. All he could do was be there for her and it was going to take time.

"I am sorry, Simon. I just didn't... *couldn't*... talk about it with you. I didn't want to spoil things... us. Can I make it up to you?"

"Yes!" Simon said instantly,

Kimberly looked up anxiously.

"A cooked breakfast!"

Kim thought out loud, "I don't have any eggs."

"No, this is big, Kim, it'll have to be a proper cooked breakfast, the full Monty. Posh breakfast at Harry's caff!"

"Alright!" she giggled, "I guess that's a very mild punishment. Tell you what, I'll get Chrissy to have Amy for an hour and we can do it properly."

*

As they walked towards the café Simon noticed a man watching them from the other side of the road.

The man looked furtively at them, glancing up and then down again.

"Is it a ghost?" he asked.

"Yes, just a ghost. They are harmless, but it's best to ignore them."

Once they reached the café, Simon stopped outside.

"Did you ever have a funeral for the family?"

Kimberly giggled, "A what?"

"You know, a proper send off, a proper..."

Kimberly gave Simon a mock Medusa stare and interrupted his flow, "I thought we'd discussed this last night, I only think of them as dead!" Simon raised an eyebrow, waiting for the idea to register. "Oh I see! Yeah, I get it." They continued along a few more steps. "Will you help me do that?"

"We can do it now. Are you Catholic or Church of England?" Simon asked, slightly surprised that he didn't know the answer.

"Protestant."

"OK, then it's St Cuthman, on Blackhawk Way, I think. We can plan our ceremony over breakfast."

*

It wasn't until midday that they finally arrived at the graveyard. It was a dark, cloudy day and the sky looked threatening, seeming to hold back its downpour. As they approached the church gates they saw a group leaving, dressed in smart, dark clothes getting into black cars. Feeling underdressed and uninvited, Simon hesitated at the gates. It was Kimberly that pushed on the gates and led them up the pathway towards the church doors. They were about to follow the path around to the graveyard when the vicar appeared as if from nowhere. They felt even more like trespassers, seeing him in his cassock and dog collar.

"Are you here for Sean Jeffries?" Simon nodded. "I'm afraid you've just missed the service. But look, if you'd like to you could still pay your respects at the grave." He pointed to the graveyard. "It's just at the front there, do you see, next to the one with the white flowers? There's no headstone of course."

Simon found his voice, "Thank you, sir, er, Father. Yup, I can see it. Thank you." They hurried to the grave.

As they approached Simon felt Kimberly's reluctance, she was falling behind. He slowed and let her overtake. She walked past the deep unfilled hole, perhaps because she knew that it was the grave of the person who'd just had his funeral. Simon reached for her hand and with the last few steps he felt it tighten and her footsteps labour. She stopped in front of the grave with white flowers. He waited for her to calm down. It took a lot longer than Simon had anticipated; perhaps she wasn't ready? He heard her sigh and felt her hand loosen. This grave was perfect. Perfect for what they needed.

"Is it OK if I say a few words?"

She nodded.

Simon cleared his throat to begin, he had been thinking of what to say since breakfast. "It's time to say goodbye to the family. Now they are all gone. We will not see them again, although we may see their ghosts. These ghosts are a link to our past, but they do not affect us now." Simon glanced at Kimberly, she was looking intensely at the grave. "We will try to remember the good times, when it all worked, and we will try and celebrate them as the stories of our lives. But now is the moment to move on and make changes and new friends. To look to the future and not to the past, which is broken and cannot be repaired. We say goodbye and blow a kiss for the love that was once there," he squeezed Kimberley's hand, "and we count our blessings that we have Amy too."

Simon hoped Kimberley would say something. But she looked oddly cold, although at least she was calm. Eventually she looked up and smiled at Simon.

"Thank you. They were the words I couldn't find. They were just right." She bent down and picked up a handful of soil and threw it on to the freshly filled grave. They stood there for a few minutes in silence.

Kim was the first to turn and Simon followed. As they walked, Simon tried to feel Kim. Had it worked? Was she released from the past? He tried to sense her from the way she held his hand and from the way she moved. Was she going to crawl out from her nightmare? Would it drag her back again?

By the time they got to the church gates Simon was ready with his question. "Kim? Is there anything here for you, anything you'd miss, in Brighton I mean?" He stopped walking and turned to hold both of her hands. "Let's go and live near my family; you said you liked Chester? I don't think we have to go as far as Norway like your grandma!"

"That would be acceptable!"

Simon heard the lighter side of Kimberly in her voice. "Amy needs a father," Simon said bluntly, "I'd like to be Amy's father."

"That would be most acceptable." Her expression was such that Simon had never seen before, her eyes somehow warmer, peaceful. He had an instant wish to see that face again.

They walked back, Kimberly was picking up the pace now and walking ahead of Simon.

"I'm sorry for your loss." It was the vicar again talking to Kimberley.

Kimberley was smiling, "Thank you, but things are working out pretty well."

Simon took over. "Er, thank you, we didn't know him that well." The path to the exit took them closer to the vicar.

"Are you new to the town?" The vicar offered out his hand.

"Simon, I forgot to say something," Kimberly interrupted, "give me a minute." Simon turned to see Kimberly walking quickly back to the grave.

"Er, kind of," Simon shook the vicar's hand, "I'm a trainee nurse at the Sussex County."

"OK, not far then! We are always keen for new attendees. Not desperate, you understand, we are one of the more popular venues. I'm actually new myself; I only took on this church a month ago. Are you a regular, Simon?" Over the vicar's shoulder, Simon saw Kimberley at the grave.

"I have to admit it's been a while, since my last visit... to church, I mean."

"Well, we are a friendly bunch here. Relatively modern, no guitars and clapping but we have been known to end a Sunday service with a cuppa and bacon butty!"

"Ah, that's my kind of church." Simon forced a smile. He saw Kimberly with her back to him her arms were in the air, swaying them from side to side.

"We also have a very well attended Sunday school. Do you have children, Simon?"

"Well, er." Simon hesitated as he saw Kimberly turn towards him and then walk back again, her hands punching the sky. "Yeah, Amy. She's not mine, but I'm going to make a go of it with Kim. I've asked her to go back with me. To Chester I mean." Simon was aware that he was gushing. He couldn't quite see what Kim was doing, but now she had stopped and her arms were no longer airborne. "I'd better go, I'm afraid. You do have a lovely church. If we do decide to stay, we'll pop along. 'Bye."

"Er, goodbye. Take care."

Simon hurried to the graveside and found his worst fears confirmed. White petals lay crushed and grubby, trodden into the soft earth. Deep footprints had made the top of the grave a complete mess. He took his place next to Kimberly. "Bloody hell, Kim!" She was silent. "Come on, let's get out of here before that vicar comes over." He tried to grab her hand but she slipped out from his grip.

"I haven't finished," she said quietly. "Mum, Dad, I've come to say goodbye. I've spent the last five years trying to work out why? Why you didn't support me. I think I know now. It's quite clear really; I just couldn't bring myself to see it. You don't love me. Perhaps you think you do, but if your love was anything like what I feel for Amy then there is nothing that I could have done that would make you turn your back on me. I don't need your love now; Amy and I are doing alright and now we have Simon. It would have been nice to have had you too, but that can never happen now. Goodbye, Dad, goodbye, Mum."

They stood like that for a minute. Simon wanted to get away and tried hard to conceal his anxiety, but looking over his shoulder for the vicar and the shuffling of his feet betrayed him. Kimberly responded and looked at Simon, she looked at her feet and she looked at the flowers. "Bloody hell, Simon!"

"Yeah! Bloody hell, Kim." Kimberly examined the earth on her shoes, and the mess she had made of the grave.

"What have I done?"

"Like, yeah!?" She looked at the flattened flowers as if it were someone else's deed.

Kimberley stood still. She looked up and around at the trees and the sky. The graveyard had a serene and strange beauty. "When can we leave?"

"Well we'd better get out of here now!"

"No, I mean for Chester?"

"As soon as you're packed."

Kimberley nodded. She pushed back her hair and tried to wipe the mud off her shoes. She turned to leave and pulled Simon by his hand, "Come on, let's go and get Amy. Let's go make our plans." And once more Simon saw Kimberley's new face: soft, mellow and open.

Luke McEwen

Listening to George

"You seldom listen to me, and when you do you don't hear, and when you do hear you hear wrong, and even when you hear right you change it so fast that it's never the same."

Marjorie Kellogg

Chapter One

Libraries shouldn't have windows, Sasha decided, *especially windows that overlook the student union bar.* How was one to concentrate?

Sasha leaned back in her chair and put her feet up on the table. Her purple Doc Martins were now acting as a paperweight on a copy of Psychology Today. She rolled her head up and scanned the ceiling as she tried to find inspiration. But the only new idea that came to mind was that the library ceiling had probably not been painted since it was first built.

The conversation on the table next to her caught Sasha's attention. The couple's discussion had become increasingly intense.

"I tell you what, I'll drive you over if you like?" said a boy wearing large headphones, a jean jacket and four day old stubble. He was perched on the table, leaning over the girl slightly as she sat in her chair.

The girl didn't say anything and was not looking at the boy; instead she was looking at the ruler that she was tapping on her pencil case.

"It's going to be a great party, Danny's coming. You know Danny, don't cha?"

The girl, still silent, continued to prop her head up with her hand, almost shielding her face from the boy.

Sasha tried to refocus on the task at hand and picked up the exam paper she had been deliberating over for the last forty minutes. It wasn't that the question was hard, it just wasn't relevant. She wanted to answer a different question.

"Look, I'll tell you what," continued the boy, now taking the ruler from the girl's hand, "forget about last night, I can make it up to you at the party. Go on, give me another chance."

Sasha turned her head now to watch the conversation as she fiddled with her nose ring. So as not to look as though she was listening she pretended to inspect the black nail polish on her fingers.

"You know I didn't mean to hurt you," the boy insisted, "I was only teasing. I didn't mean to push so hard, you know that, don't you babe?"

Sasha looked back at the exam paper. *It must be some kind of riddle,* she thought, *this stupid question wants me to argue something which isn't completely true.* As her eyes found the ceiling again she tried to picture the scene of the person who had managed to write some graffiti next to the light fitting. She soon concluded, *I'm not getting anywhere, time for a drink!*

She packed up her patchwork handbag and stood up to leave.

"Go on, I'll get you a pizza before we go, you can get the beers, what do you say?" The boy was now buckled over, trying to get the girl to look at him.

As Sasha strolled past the couple she felt somehow irritated that she had not heard the girl's side of the story. Why hadn't the girl spoken up? she thought, and with that she turned on her heel and walked back to the boy.

She pulled at the boy's headphones, letting them snap back.

"Are these too loud?" Sasha asked, keeping her voice quiet but severe.

"They're not on!" the boy protested, and winced at the pain from his ear.

"Well, it's just that you don't seem to be hearing anything she's saying," Sasha continued.

"She wasn't saying anything," the boy explained, incredulous at the assault.

"So, we've established that you can hear, but you didn't seem to be understanding. Let me translate!" She turned directly towards him and inched closer. "She doesn't want to go out with you tonight. She's pissed that you hurt her and she doesn't want to talk to you," Sasha's voice began to raise, "why don't you back off, give her some space and work out what you should really be saying."

Sasha wasn't sure if she'd gone too far, but she looked at the girl who mouthed, "Thank you," from behind her hand.

The boy stood up but Sasha stood her ground and stared him in the eye. He rose to his full height and Sasha tried to remember if there was anything behind her should she step back. He must have been over six feet and dwarfed Sasha, but she was determined not to flinch. The boy just looked at her stone-faced, momentarily holding his stare and then walked off at a somewhat overly protracted pace.

Sasha relaxed her shoulders and focused to slow the momentum of her racing heart. "I'm going to the bar if you fancy a drink?" she offered quietly.

"I'm OK," the girl said, "I'm just going to think for a while, but thanks for that." She forced a smile at Sasha but looked quite forlorn.

*

The bar was relatively full, but not too noisy with it being late in the afternoon. Sasha chose a seat by the window, ironically she found herself staring back at the library. She sipped her coffee and once again picked up the paper that was giving her so much frustration.

"Hey, Sash!"

Sasha looked up. It was Dermot, a popular boy from her dorm. "Hey you, what's up?" she replied.

"Nothing's up, it's pants! I've got three essays to write by the end of the week…"

"Well, I've just got the one," Sasha interrupted, "due on Friday, but I can't get going. I have to write five thousand words in just two days!"

He sat next to her with his knees and torso facing her, his arm extended along the back of the sofa. "Yeah, well it can't be as bad as, 'Compare and contrast the changes to Trade Union philosophy to the rise and fall of membership pre and post Thatcherism,' can it?" Dermot spoke the title of his essay by putting on a received English accent and ending it with a yawn.

Sasha didn't respond. *Yes,* she thought, *that did sound dreadfully dull.*

"Go on then, give me your title, how bad can it be? You're doing Applied Psychology, yeah?" Dermot asked as he raised an eyebrow.

"Yup, the counselling module." She then responded with the same posh accent. "'Empathy is a vital element in communication and the most important skill in a counsellor's tool box, discuss in five thousand words'."

"I could blag that for you," Dermot insisted, "no worries. Everyone knows that empathy is the most important thing. If you want to get on with someone then you must let them know that you know exactly how they're feeling. If you can sympathise and show people you have compassion for what they're going through, they'll open up to you!" Dermot was quite animated and he felt sure that he could help out. "When do you need it done by?"

"By Friday!" Sasha said, in a tone that let him know that she had already told him. She smiled and gave him a cheeky grin. Dermot grinned back and nodded, registering acceptance of his error. He became quiet, trying to show her that he would be more attentive.

"Well..." she paused, "...I'm not so sure! I've given it a lot of thought and I think the question is barking up the wrong tree. Empathy is important. It can show someone that you understand what they are going through. It enables you to recognise someone's emotions and it helps you to respond accordingly..." she paused, waiting for Dermot to catch-up, "...you know, with an appropriate tone of voice. You need to understand what emotions they are struggling with, whether it be fear, anxiety or anger, then you can help them identify those emotions in themselves and help them work through those emotions, but..." she paused, looking at Dermot's fingers, which were repeatedly pulling his hair around behind his ear, "...in fact, I've read that counsellors can have too much empathy and that they can become affected by the client's emotions, which doesn't help the client. You can feel and share someone's emotions," she hesitated as she formulated her argument," but if you get too involved it can become an emotional roller-coaster! That would be exhausting! A counsellor wants someone to open up so that they can see how they feel, but they shouldn't get lost in that person's emotions." Dermot was looking at Sasha from behind his coffee cup, lost in her words. Feeling its rim with his tongue. "They need to be there for that person, they should stay fully present to what they are saying and their body language. The moment is all about the client and how they feel, not about how the counsellor feels when they hear their stories. Therefore, I would say that being a good listener is more important."

"Oh yeah, yeah," Dermot agreed enthusiastically, "if you want to get the girl into bed, you gotta do the listening. You need to know what her likes and dislikes are." He grinned as he flicked a lock of golden hair from his eyes.

Sasha feigned an irritated tut, although actually she quite liked the idea of Dermot wanting to know more about her.

"OK, Mr Political Science, thank you for your deep input," she mocked, "what if the girl doesn't know what she likes? What if all you read from her face is that she's interested, but you don't know why she's interested? Does she want to be friends or does she want to be more than friends?" She raised an eyebrow. She noticed that he had shaved that morning and that he had been sneaking glances at her chest while she was talking.

"Now you've got me there, Sasha. To know the mind of a woman, you do need to be a woman!"

"No!" Sasha retorted, "that's the point. The most important tool in my tool box is the ability to listen. Listening! Using these two instruments," she said, whilst rubbing her earlobes. She paused, waiting for Dermot to make eye contact. He seemed to be more focused on what it would be like to give her earlobe a little nibble. "If I could give you all my attention and without any assumption or judgment, comprehend totally what you are saying, perhaps I would know you more fully than you know yourself."

Dermot was now quiet, his jaw dropped and his eyes focused intently on Sasha's stare. Sasha suspected that if she'd said that the most important tool in her toolbox was a spanner, he might have agreed.

"What if," Sasha continued, "I could so fully concentrate on what you're saying, I could listen to your voice, your tone, your words, read between the lines and observe every subtle movement that your body makes, that I could then know the right questions to ask, and uncover truths that you weren't even aware of! I could uncover all your desires and fantasies. What a useful tool that would be?" She grinned with excitement.

"That would be bloody terrifying!" Dermot bellowed, "no one's going hear about my fantasies!"

In the moment of shared laughter that followed, Sasha realised that she would procrastinate a little more before starting her essay.

Chapter Two

The counsellor had not slept well and was apprehensive about today's meeting. She reminded herself to start with an open mind and to begin, as always, by seeking understanding. If she could overcome the inherent obstacles of clear communication in this unusual meeting, then success was possible.

For that, she contemplated, was the basis of any good relationship: good, clear and honest communication. A willingness to be open and exchange knowledge of each other's fears and passions. A motivation to make a connection between the physical and spiritual universal truths that threaten to separate everyone. How her current clients achieved that in their everyday existence she was unsure, but was fascinated to find out.

She didn't have much background information in regards to their particular circumstances. She knew they needed marriage guidance and that they had been together a long time. Marriage guidance was her speciality; however, whenever she started a new case she was always overwhelmed with apprehension. Clients always assumed that they needed some kind of reconciliation but she found that, more often than not, they merely needed permission to let go and move on.

*

The counsellor drew in a deep breath and stiffened her shoulders, bringing an air of formality to the proceedings. "So let's get started, shall we? Can I begin by taking a few personal details please, what are your full names?"

"We are George and Lucy Fairfaxe. I am the squire of Broadwood Manor, Suffolk."

"Date of birth?"

"Mine is the sixteenth of August 1838, Lucy's is the twelfth of April 1852."

"And what is your relationship to each other?"

"We are married."

"And what are you looking for in today's meeting, what is the problem that you would like to resolve?"

"My wife and I have been happily married for many years, but just recently things have changed and we'd like a little help with that. Wouldn't we, dear?"

The counsellor noted that Lucy had not replied to George. "OK, can you begin by giving me some background information about your relationship, how did you meet?"

"I first properly noticed Lucy at church. Of course, I would have known of her a long time before then since we always go to church on a Sunday. We have done so our whole lives. I would have been in the same church as Lucy from when she was just a baby, but I didn't really take an interest in her until she started to become a young woman. I can remember when she was thirteen, perhaps twelve, her fine features. She was delicate, with long hair, slender fingers and a clear complexion; she was a real beauty of a lass. And although the daughter of a herdsmen, she always turned herself out well. She kept her clothes clean and her hair neatly braided.

I can remember her giggling in the back row when I entered the church. I caught her eye as if to hush her up since she shouldn't be giggling in church. I was expecting her to be embarrassed, but she gave me a cheeky nod. I noticed then that she was developing a womanly figure and I have to say that I took a fancy to her there and then.

At the time my father's health had taken a turn for the worse and he required me to spend much more time managing the farm. I had suspended my studies to pay more attention to the farm and, although earlier than perhaps I should, I thought it was time to take on a wife. When I heard that Lucy would be leaving for London to enter service as soon as she turned fourteen, I approached her father and sought Lucy's hand."

The counsellor had grown increasingly aware that the conversation was a little one-sided, she wanted to include Lucy. "How did you feel about that, Lucy, were you anxious about leaving your family to work?"

"I can't remember being worried about it..." Lucy paused, "...it might have been exciting."

"I had seen Lucy playing with the other girls," George continued with his monologue, "when she helped out at the Sunday school before the ten o'clock service. She had a lovely way about her. She would keep the other girls in order yet she would be kind and supportive. I remember her laughing with them and thought then what a lovely girl to have as my wife. She would pick up the ways of the manor house quite quickly, and would become a suitable lady and mother to bring up my children.

There was the time I saw her when she played Mary in the nativity, I think she must have been thirteen. She held the little baby with such tenderness and grace. There were other children from the village in the play, but they were mucking around a little. In particular was the boy who played Joseph, a foolish little lad, and Lucy managed to keep him in check with a quick and severe stare. I think he may have had a little crush on Lucy for he was very alert to her. He stood up straight and did as he should for the rest of the play.

But the little incident made me pay heed that Lucy was indeed ready for marital union."

The counsellor reflected on Lucy's long brown hair, beautiful eyes and wonderful figure, it struck her that George had done quite well for himself. It really was time to bring her back into the conversation. "I'm sorry to interrupt, can I just confirm, was it at that time, Lucy, that George asked you to marry him?"

George didn't give Lucy time to answer. "It wasn't the custom at the time," George hesitated, reflecting on why the counsellor had asked the question. "It would not have been appropriate for me to ask Lucy, I hardly knew her. But once Lucy's father had given his approval I arranged to have Lucy and her family over to the Manor for afternoon tea. Lucy and I got a bit of time to speak then."

"How did that go?" The counsellor was unable to disguise the intrigue in her tone, she would have loved to have watched the meeting. How did Lucy cope, she would have been so young as she watched her life being arranged in front of her, as part of an negotiation between George and her father.

George pondered the question, it was a long time ago. "Well, I think it was quite awkward for Lucy's family. I remember Lucy's father was very quiet, her mother did most of the talking. I don't think they'd been to a drawing room before. I did the best I could to make them feel welcome. I think getting out the fine china wasn't a great idea since Lucy's father was terrified of breaking it. They hadn't had tea before and I think Lucy's father would have been more at home with a jar of ale. Forgive me, Lucy, I don't want to sound unkind, but it was a difficult hour.

I think Lucy's father was more concerned about the effect that it would have on his work as herdsman, he wouldn't have Lucy to help, after we married. I had not thought of any changes to the running of the estate, so I managed to deal with his fears quite easily. In fact, I suggested that Lucy's father should take on the fallow paddock at the back of lower meadow. It made good sense for it to be used and I settled the proposal on the understanding that he wouldn't interfere with the hunt as it passed over his crop. In previous years he'd tried to block our passage."

"But what of Lucy, George, what was said?"

George was quiet, deliberating what the question meant. It was Lucy that eventually explained, "He didn't go down on one knee if that's what you mean," Lucy giggled, "it wasn't like that between us, I hardly knew him then."

"OK, but how was the question put to you?" The counsellor persisted, wondering now if Lucy had ever given her approval or acceptance.

"Well, that was easily dealt with. I think Lucy wasn't looking forward to going to London and leaving her family behind. Her father had told her of my proposal so there was little to be agreed. I asked her if she would be my wife in the Manor house and she accepted readily. She seemed more concerned as to what her chores would be. I think she thought she'd have to carry on helping her father with the milking and then return and do all the housework at the Manor house. When I told her that we had people in service to help with the housework she didn't really take it in. She was comforted though when I confirmed that she could help them, should she wish."

"Well, thank you for the background, George, now can we come to the issue of what is wrong now. You said things had changed recently, can you recall what happened to make things change?"

"Oh yes, that's not difficult at all, it was the day William Wallace was purchased."

"Excuse me, William Wallace?"

"Yes," George confirmed, "commander in the Scottish Wars of Independence, he died 1305. Wallace defeated an English army at the Battle of Stirling Bridge in 1297, and was Guardian of Scotland, serving until his defeat at the Battle of Falkirk in July 1298..."

The counsellor interrupted, "I don't understand, sorry, why are you talking about William Wallace?"

"That was the day Lucy's and my relationship changed. We had been happily living together for a hundred and seventy-five years, until William was purchased and placed next to us. Little Red Riding Hood was placed on the lower shelf to our right, she was a charming young girl, I might add..."

"No, please stop, what are you talking about? I don't understand, I thought you owned a farm and lived in Suffolk, who are these people that you share your house with?" The counsellor was now quite perplexed.

"Little Red Riding Hood is just part of the collection. She was purchased about the same time as Lucy and I. She's not entirely genuine, I'd say she's more Edwardian. Whereas Lucy and I are the real thing. Manufactured in Staffordshire in 1852, then sold at a market fair in 1853. Genuine Staffordshire flat back figurines.

Lucy and I stand joined together as we have always done, a double character figurine, one single piece of clay. Dressed in our Sunday best, with my arm around the bouquet that was made for us on our engagement.

Lucy's holding a basket of fruit from her father's fields, representing our life ahead full of prosperity."

For the first time there was silence. The counsellor, applying her training and not making a judgement, decided to follow her curiosity.

"And how is it that William's arrival changed things for you both?"

For the first time George was a little reticent to talk. "Well, it's a little awkward," he said finally.

"Try to elaborate, was it something he said?" she probed.

George reluctantly continued, "It's not what he says, it's more how he says it. Well no, it's just him bloody being there. Sorry, I didn't mean to... Well, I didn't want to..." George didn't finish his sentence.

The counsellor waited for George to continue.

"Lucy and I have always been close. It may not be everyone's idea of intimacy but we have been inseparable for so long. This William scoundrel is getting in the way of our routine, our closeness."

"Is that how you feel, Lucy?" the counsellor enquired.

George continued, "He's just so uncouth, the man doesn't know how to conduct himself. We belong to a fine collection. I gather from what has been said that together we are worth in excess of twelve hundred guineas, that's equivalent to ten years of rent I collected from the estate. This William fellow was bought off eBay and is quite clearly some modern copy. His glaze is too glossy, clearly made from porcelain and not pottery, and his features are too fine. You only need to look at his nose, it's far too defined for a Fairing."

"He may be a reproduction, George, but he is well made, he'd survive a fall quite well, I think." Lucy had interrupted the conversation for the first time and George became silent.

The silence became uncomfortable.

"And, George, other than threatening the integrity of the collection, what are your concerns with William?" the counsellor persisted.

George was silent and struggled to find an answer that was polite. He huffed and sighed with frustration.

"What is it about William that has caused your relationship with Lucy to change?"

George sucked in his breath as if drawing in his strength to speak. He wanted to explode with his thoughts, but he kept his metre even and managed a smooth explanation.

"They talk all the time with each other. They talk about what is going on in the room, about the decorations, about the other figurines, about what is on the radio and the television. They are always laughing together and his sense of humour is quite uncouth. I don't like the way he influences Lucy, the things he says when speaking with her are just not Lucy, it's as though he's turning her into some kind of loose woman. I'm sure I have heard the others laughing at what she says, laughing at her, not with her! She's been talking about me and our time together. I don't see that it's Lucy's place to do that, and I think William shouldn't be encouraging her."

"OK, I can hear you're quite anxious about that, what is it about their talking that upsets you?"

George was perplexed, surely he'd just explained that. Suddenly he felt tired, his energy seemed to have drained from him. Perhaps this counselling was a bad idea. What did he hope to achieve? Lucy didn't really seem to understand either. She was just so young, how could she understand his difficulty? As head of the house, a figurehead to the village, an equal to the Rector, could she not see that her new friendship was a challenge to all of that?

"What is it that you would have changed?" the counsellor pushed.

"Put the scoundrel on a lower shelf!" George blurted out, "put him far away from Lucy and me. He doesn't belong with us, he's a cheap fake and a bad influence. Look at his record. Hung drawn and quartered, what an end for anyone! He was a cattle rustler and traitor to the state. I can't stand the way he is dusted almost every day and how he is presented to visitors as 'one of the finest in the collection'. It's nonsense, why can't everyone see him for the phoney that he is?"

"He is not a traitor, he is loyal to Scotland, not England, that's all," Lucy said quietly but firmly, "he is well travelled, a brilliant military strategist and a brave man."

Each of these points was as if an arrow was cutting into George's heart. He winced as she made each point.

"And as for daily polishing," Lucy continued, "I gather that we have become too fragile to be dusted daily. George, you are getting old and you need to accept that." Lucy was firm, yet she tried not to be patronising.

George was mortified at Lucy's last onslaught, *of all the things she could have said!*

George had been dropped. It was one of the children who was to blame. A Christmas toy had been fired at him and it had knocked George and Lucy off the shelf. But it was George who had taken the impact. They had landed on his head and now he had a white chip in it, as well as a fracture down his back. They had bounced and then landed precariously on top of a hoover, where further damage was caused to the glazing on his loose breeches.

This ignominious fall had had a far greater impact on George than the physical scars that detracted from his value. The owner of the collection was horrified at the consequences of their child's play. The Lord and Lady had been the centre of the collection, their most prized possession. But valuations and professional opinion had concluded that a repair was neither desirable nor economical and it was best to live with the impairment. They would never hold the same position in the collection that they once did. Although Lucy was unharmed and as beautiful as she always had been, the fall had been a blow to her self-worth too.

Whereas once they were presented to visitors and admired by them, especially other collectors, Lucy felt now as though she may as well be at the back of the shelf. George had done well to survive for so long, they both had. They had survived all the journeys they had made, from the factory to the fairground, and then to all the homes they had been in. But now time had caught up with them. She accepted that nothing in life lasts forever and circumstances beyond their control had led to their demise. It was as predictable as the sun coming over the horizon, their end was in sight, for they had seen it with so many of the others. Once damaged, visitors never handled them with as much care. It was highly likely that more damage would ensue.

There were so many future possibilities but none of them better than where they had been. They had had their heyday, their moment in the sun, and now the future looked bleak. Chipped figurines were often held in the collection for sentimental reasons, "They are part of the family," they had often heard. But when future purchases were made, the owners would make room.

Be it on an online auction, a sale to another collector, a donation to a charity shop or, worse still, to be boxed in the attic. Too valuable to be thrown away but not good enough to be sold. Their days in a box could be long, it might as well be forever, and for Lucy, the other loss would be her friendship with the others.

To Lucy, George had always been a kind man, fair and loyal, of good heart and a pillar of virtue in the community. But as the years passed and she came into contact with others, she was excited by their stories, their experiences and the things they loved. Many of them were full of passion and had had amazing adventures. She'd stood opposite Rob Roy in a shop once, for over a week in fact. He was such an interesting man and he'd fought in many battles. He'd won many but been severely wounded in others. He'd protected his mother when his father was in prison. He'd lost everything in business to someone entrusted with his purse, and his family and children and been evicted from their home.

Then there was Dr Syntax, who travelled the country looking for beauty. He was a peripatetic clergyman and would speak endlessly of his adventures, such as his run in with a highwayman and the time he was chased by a bull. Once he had mistakenly walked into someone's house thinking it was an inn. He had many mishaps, from being robbed at the races to being thrown from a carriage and horse. He was so amusing, even if he did smoke and drink a little too much.

Lucy loved to hear of the things that she hadn't experienced, she often wondered if life would have been better if she had left the village and gone into service in London.

The counsellor coughed, hopping to bring some focus to the conversation, "George, Lucy doesn't share your opinion of William, can you accept that?"

George deliberated.

"Can you allow Lucy to have her own views, to follow her own destiny?"

George remained silent.

"How would it be if you had been placed next to a beautiful lady figurine, do you think Lucy would have felt jealous?"

"I'm not jealous," George protested, "I've already said William is just a cad, an imposter. He's not one of us that's all, he's no more than twenty years old."

"What does that matter?" interrupted Lucy, "Jack and Jill were quite clearly reproductions."

"Can we leave the children out of this?" George retorted firmly.

It had been the happiest time for Lucy, having Jack and Jill arrive next to them so early on in their marriage. Her whole life fell into place and it gave the richest contentment to the context in which George and Lucy were bound together. Their dreams and marriage made sense. Jack and Jill interlaced with all aspects of their lives. The children were inseparable. Locked in eternal youth, they were always joyful, hopeful and playful. It was a wonderful distraction for Lucy, and for George it was a proud moment to have the family he'd planned for.

Their routine was perfect. Lucy would wake the children at six forty-five a.m. and start with morning prayers. They would plan their day on the farm, including what fields should be sown, ploughed or harvested, as well as which of the cattle should be sired and which taken to market. Jack showed great promise in his interest in the new-fangled farm machinery.

Lucy and Jill would plan their day with cooking. They would decide together what recipes to try out, whether to take trips to the market or the field to collect ingredients. George and Jack would discuss the farm accounts, such as which rents could be increased and whether to sell the corn or store it for higher prices. They would always get together in the evening to play word games or have a family sing-song. Jack and Jill loved their parlour games.

Lucy would tell the children about her days in the milking parlour. About the time a stubborn old cow would not let her milk her and was forever kicking the bucket over. About her time in Sunday school, when she had been given responsibilities to teach the children but often played with them instead.

George would instruct the family, Jack in particular, in the ways of squiredom. The proper conduct at the harvest festival, church fetes and how to handle the men. His favourite story to recount was how he and his father had caught a tenant red-handed poaching from the estate, and how they had pardoned him in exchange for rebuilding the farm's perimeter wall.

For Lucy, Jill would grow up to have the life that she had not had. She loved it when one of the other figurines was close by so that Jill could hear all their exciting stories of adventure. Jill would travel and she would have time to discover herself before she settled down to marriage. Hopefully she would find someone like George, but who had perhaps explored the world a bit more.

George, although pleased with Jack's development, felt that Jack did not have the personality required to run the farm and the wider estate. Often he seemed more likely destined for the circus than the responsibilities of animal husbandry and crop rotation.

Many years passed in this way, indeed how quickly twenty years passed before the family were divided. Lucy took it the hardest. She had never spent much time thinking about the time when it would just be George and her on their own again. It all happened quite suddenly. Jack and Jill were there in the evening and then gone in the morning. They had been replaced over night with another Jack and Jill figurine. Apparently the new arrivals were more valuable, being authentic and having a distinguished provenance of being owned by a famous antique expert who was always on TV.

Their relationship with the new Jack and Jill was not the same. They tried hard to make it so, but Jack and Jill just didn't seem very receptive.

The counsellor finally disturbed the silence. "George, what are your real fears about Lucy's relationship with William?"

"The man's a cad and he's changing her," George said desperately, "I love Lucy, I don't want things to change, I don't want to lose her..."

"George?" Lucy interrupted softly, "thank you, George, it is the first time you have said that."

The counsellor waited for Lucy's statement to register with George before continuing with the session. "But I don't understand, how can things change when you are physically joined?" The counsellor's question was almost rhetorical, she was intrigued as to what George was frightened off.

"At night," George continued more coolly, "and I may be wrong, forgive me Lucy if it is my dreams haunting me, but I think I hear you whispering with William."

"Stop!" Lucy exclaimed, "please, please do not continue, you don't need to worry. I don't know what you heard. I can assure you that I have never spoken to William while you were asleep. George, please know that you don't need to worry. I'm sorry I didn't tell you before but William has been sold and he's leaving tomorrow." Lucy recovered, realising that she should have just stopped this conversation long ago.

Again, an awkward silence ensued.

"So, George, are you happy?" the counsellor questioned, "does that allay your fears?"

"No!" George said, brooding, "something has been lost. I agree that the future is more certain, but…"

"Is the future ever certain, George?" the counsellor interrupted, "what is left, George? I'm hearing that you harbour some resentment."

There was a stony silence and George's face gradually reddened. The counsellor and Lucy waited for George's reply and, like a volcano, they waited for its big eruption.

"Did you desire him!?" George was now loud and spitting out his words. "Did you want that man, did you ever want me? Did you ever want me like you wanted him?" George's voice raised to a crescendo.

There it was, all his fears out in the open, clearly stated for the record. They could never be unsaid. George sensed the weight of future decades, the many moments that would remind him of his outspoken self-doubt and lack of faith in Lucy. How he would torment himself with the memory that he had questioned her loyalty after all this time together.

In that moment George's tortured mind flexed the rigid structure of his being. He felt the molecules of his soul as the stress of his angst pushed him to oblivion. The crack down his back, which started on top of his chipped head, threatened to win the battle against his mind's desire to stay in one piece. George imagined himself shattered and broken. His head lying fragmented on the floor and his body strewn about on the shelf.

Lucy felt George's torture like an earthquake and imagined clearly for the first time a picture of her life alone, knowing full well in that instant what her fate would be.

"No, George," Lucy shouted, "keep it together, we are one. We are part of each other. You know that, it is how we are designed. We are inseparable, do not ever stop believing in that! I will love you forever." She lowered her voice, "Stop this. Stop this constant worrying. We will have our ups and down, but together we will always be."

George calmed down. His soul soothed by Lucy's words. He felt her now, he felt her inside him. They had reconnected and the torture slowly released itself, dissipating the decades of accumulated fear and anxiety.

"Say it again, Lucy," George whispered, "tell me you love me."

Chapter Three

Dermot's head lay on Sasha's bare chest as the sunlight streamed through the bedroom window, lighting up the dust particles like a Broadway production.

"So, how did that essay go anyway?" Dermot said quietly, "did the lecturer go for your listening tool thing?"

"An 'A' star," Sasha answered, "he loved my exposition of me as a counsellor meeting with an inanimate object." She paused, stroking Dermot's hair. "It was easy to imagine what the figurines might say and feel, but it was the exchange between the counsellor and the figurines which made the meeting believable." She felt Dermot snuggle into her as though wanting to hear more. "The counsellor was listening and it was that which allowed her to help them with their relationship. She listened without judging. Often people just need to feel like they have been listened to, that their pains have been heard, and after that their emotions that they have been holding onto start to fade away. But only once they truly feel like they have been heard, no matter how bizarre their story is!" She giggled and then paused as she imagined the two figurines talking to her in the meeting. "The lecturer said some lovely things, actually, that I should consider counselling as a career. My skills in listening combined with my existentialist approach to the human condition," she said with a posh voice, "and my willingness to want to understand other people would make me a good counsellor. But he did say don't do it for the wrong reasons, like if you think it's easy money, or you just like talking to people. If that's the case then perhaps it's not the right role for you."

"Oh right, excellent. Well done you!" Dermot was elated. "I'd be bowled over with an 'A' star. Was it unusual then, your argument, were you saying stuff that no one else was saying? What was the right answer?" Dermot was wondering if having a bright girlfriend would rub off on him.

"I don't know," Sasha giggled, "but I do know he fancies me!" And with that she tickled Dermot under the arm and laughed hysterically during the ensuing play fight.

"Wait, wait!" Dermot pleaded, holding her hand away from his armpit, and putting his face right up to hers. "How do you know he fancies you?"

"Because he read my essay," she smiled "he properly read it! He said that I do the same cheeky nod that Lucy did to George in the church, but to him!" She watched Dermot's eyes for his reaction, as she contemplated the lecturer holding her essay and re-reading it perhaps once too often.

"The dirty old man!" Dermot said laughing. "Well, I'm the one who got the girl!" And with that he found the ticklish part of Sasha's neck, he gently bit it, while not letting go of her hands and made Sasha squeal with delight.

Listening to George

The Thimble

In his book, titled *Collecting: An Unruly Passion: Psychological Perspectives,* Muensterberger says that control of the object collected brings, "Relief of the child's anxiety and frustration that comes with feeling helpless and being alone."

Chapter One

Anna and her father stood in front of the thimble collection, contemplating its future.

Quietly she breathed in deeply, and then released the air slowly as she tried to relax. Anna needed to concentrate on the task of the day; it was important that she carried out her responsibilities. The uncertainty of how her father would be had made her anxious about leaving home that morning. Would her father be talkative or would conversation dry up? After all, it had been a family joke about Dad's tendency to immediately pass the phone to Mum when she telephoned home, as though a daughter-mother relationship was all that existed.

"Would your kids like it, Anna?" Ted said as he folded his arms. Anna sighed and took a step closer to the main unit. She was worried about hurting her father's feelings but felt she should get straight to the point.

"There's no room at home for it, Dad, and I don't think they're really into this sort of thing. Susan and Emily don't really collect anything. But, why don't you want to keep it?" As she asked the question, she knew the answer. Her father didn't want the collection any more than she did.

It was an impressive collection, some three hundred thimbles, with a great range of styles, colours and sizes. They were made from many different materials: porcelain, steel, brass, wood, and glass, even whalebone. Some were antique, others quite modern. There were those that were made only for collecting, with the names of towns and cities written on them, while others were inscribed with the names of family members. All the thimbles were framed and displayed on the chimney side of the lounge. They were set out on a specially made shelf, with part of the collection behind glass in a deep-set frame. Custom-made lighting had been installed, with separate switches for each cabinet and a dimmer for the corner unit.

It seemed as though this was the first time that they had ever really thought about whether they actually liked it or not. For it had always been there, growing slowly from year to year. It was nothing to do with Anna or her father, it was Mum's—June's—collection. It was she who had added to the collection, one thimble at a time. A holiday purchase, a birthday present or a chance buy at a car boot sale. It had been her thing, her defining interest.

It all started when she was only eight years old. She had left home because of the war; she had been an evacuee. In those days people didn't really have many possessions. She was only allowed to take a few things anyway and one of them was her mother's thimble, the one that her grandmother had used at school when sewing classes were still part of a child's education. During her time away it was one of the few things she had had to remind herself of her mother.

Upon her return home, the next addition had been a doll's house thimble, which was so incredibly small that it had sparked off many a conversation. Her father had found it on a bombsite when he was billeted to London. It had been swiftly followed by a present from the village where she had been an evacuee, not from her host family, but from an old woman she hardly knew. The thimble had 'Beccles' painted on the side, the name of the town where she had been evacuated to. June had been surprised by the delivery for there was only a brief note with it—'Love is a daily practise', which confused everyone. Mum and Dad had said it was probably a song title. It had arrived with mixed blessings for she preferred not to dwell on her wartime experiences.

As she had begun to display the thimbles on the mantelpiece, her family had wanted to take an interest in her enjoyment. They had bought her thimbles to add to her collection. By the time she was twelve she had an impressive thirty thimbles, enough to fill her first cabinet. They did look so beautiful, neatly laid out in decreasing sizes for everyone to see.

"No, Anna, it's not really my thing either. I can't say that I'll ever have the time to dust it." Ted picked up a silver thimble and held it up to the light. "I bought this for your mother on our engagement. She teased me rotten, you know. She said it was the least romantic thing she could think of." Ted smiled as he remembered. June had kissed him softly, then put her arms around him and wouldn't let go for over a minute.

He had known she would like it, since she collected thimbles, but her reaction surpassed his expectation. It was as if he'd handed her a key to eternal happiness. "But I know that really she loved it, she loved it more than the ring we bought. She always dusts this one first, you just watch the next time..." Ted's voice trailed off to a whisper, he only just managed to finish his sentence before he turned away towards the window.

"What time are we collecting Mum?" Anna asked, attempting to change the conversation.

"They wouldn't give me a time. I told June we'd come and bring her lunch if she didn't call before twelve." Ted looked at his watch, "the problem with her hospital sessions is that she never knows how busy the hospital is going to be. You'd think they'd be able to give her a more definite time." Anna glanced at her father, she was worried he would work himself up as he'd done before, when he had lambasted the receptionist at the doctor's surgery for not giving her an appointment that day. 'Do you know she could die!' he'd exclaimed.

"It's not as though she has much energy to really wait around in there, she'd far rather be at home. She's not a patient patient." Ted looked back at the collection. "Well, if you don't want it we could sell it?"

Anna spotted the blue thimble from Portugal that she'd bought her. She remembered the mini saga of buying it. They couldn't find a thimble anywhere, but she had wanted to take something back for her mother. After all, it had been her mother who had paid for the holiday. Mum was so difficult to buy for, she didn't like to drink and didn't really have many hobbies. She had enjoyed her family and her homemaking, but after so many decades the house was just so. Buying her an ornament never really worked. It would never get displayed since her taste was too specific. But a little thimble was always readily received. Received with a hug, a smile and an, "Oh, you are so thoughtful, that is lovely!" Then another hug and a kiss.

"I don't think we'd get much for it, Dad," Anna said, almost without thinking, "eBay might work, I could ask David to put it on. It's sure to sell, of course, but I don't know how we'd get it to them, to the buyer I mean, I guess they'd have to collect it."

There was a silence as Ted pondered the practicalities of boxing up the collection and how it would be best photographed. How would you describe such a collection? Were there in fact some notable pieces that were quite valuable and should be mentioned or perhaps sold separately? He knew that he couldn't ask June about the collection and the details that he would need in order to sell it. She wouldn't understand that no one in the family really wanted it.

"OK, Anna, well let's just see what happens..." Ted paused again, working out what he would do with the wall, the gap in the décor, when it had gone. Would he just paint over it or put a picture in its place? It was June who would usually make that decision. She did all the decorating in the house. He considered himself a very lucky man to have found a wife who he loved and who was happy to decorate the home, leaving him free to concentrate on his career and his golf. She had worked hard when Anna and Carrie were growing up. She had been the mother that any child would have wished for, always arranging things for the family to do together. Never letting herself go and always presenting herself beautifully. Oh yes, he had been lucky to have found her.

It had been by chance that they had met. It wasn't as though they had any mutual friends, they had just met on a train and struck up a conversation. They had both found themselves laughing at a dog on the train, who was eagerly attracting attention from all passers-by. Ted had told June about the misdeeds of his own Jack Russell terrier, who he had owned as a boy, which included him repeatedly trying to defend the house at all cost from the invading postman. They reached agreement straight away that 'dogs were great, but better when they were someone else's'. By the time that they arrived in London they had realised that they were both living in Reading, and Ted had asked if he could take her to the flicks, the cinema, that Friday. She had thought him very cheeky but had said yes on the condition she was home by ten-thirty p.m.

He had contemplated in the past how different his life would have been if she had not sat next to him. They had grown so much together and they had complemented each other perfectly. He was ambitious in his career and had enjoyed the hard work, the hard work that was necessary for him to have achieved his place in the boardroom. He had retired many years ago and they enjoyed the wealth together that his career had brought them. June had loved her place in the family, providing solutions for her children's and husband's problems, mending things in the house when it was required, and planning summer holidays. She carried out and enjoyed the simple chores that some would have found tedious. She seemed to relish the big juggling act of keeping everything in place and just so.

The silence was broken with the chirp of an incoming text.

"Is that yours, Anna?"

"No, Dad, it's your phone!" Anna giggled.

Ted took the phone from his pocket and held it up to let the light from the window fall onto the display, "It's your mum, 'DON'T FORGET TO CANCEL THE SUNDAY TIMES, SPEAK SOON – XXX'." Ted had played with the sound of the kisses as he read them out, and with the final kiss he lowered his tone to sound romantic.

Anna smiled at her father and they were silent again as they turned to the collection. In their silence they had agreed that they didn't know what to do and therefore just to leave it unresolved, to an undetermined time when future events may present a solution.

She hesitated, wondering if it was the right time to approach the dreaded question, to tackle the main purpose of her visit today. Dad needed sorting. There were some big changes ahead and she would need to take over from Mum. Having started with their discussion of the collection, it did seem OK to continue with other important matters. "What will you do then, Dad? Move? Downsize? You could come and live with the family and me, you know that, don't you?" As she said it Anna felt that the idea was an affirmation, it was the best way of ensuring her father would be alright. She accepted the responsibility of caring for her father but only on her terms. Mum had made too many sacrifices; she'd given up her job with the Milk Marketing Board when she'd fallen pregnant with Anna. Anna had always grown up with the feeling that she would want more from her own life.

Ted briefly looked at his feet and turned to Anna. "Thank you. Let's see what happens, hey? Early days and all that."

"But what about all these things?" Anna said, meaning the furniture, the knick-knacks, the house and all of its contents. Each room was filled with twenty-six years of history, the endless shopping, sorting, placing and arranging of stuff. Furniture from shops that had been bargained for, packaged, delivered, unpacked, placed and rearranged. Ornaments that had been loved, used, and admired, as well as all the possessions that had been unloved, ignored and boxed or placed in a cupboard.

As Ted remained silent, Anna realised that, in fact, it had not been the right time to ask. "Sorry, Dad," she turned to him, "let's take Mum her lunch."

As she prepared her mum's sandwich, the house seemed to be powerfully silent. The kitchen, a room that had seen so many gatherings and was once a place of loud laughter and enthusiastic chatter, seemed to be overwhelmingly quiet now. She considered her plan. Having Dad with her would make it easier to balance all the demands on her time. Her plan to follow her career in medical research would not be compromised. Why hadn't Mum wanted that for herself? Her devotion to them was too much; she'd left nothing for herself. That was why the thimble collection didn't make sense to Anna, why she had quietly regarded it with disdain her whole life. Mum had so little 'me time', yet she chose to spend it on that. It seemed absurd. "A ridiculous waste of time," she had told husband privately.

As Anna contemplated her mother's belongings and the process of de-cluttering, she felt that she wanted to make a start on organising it all now. The house seemed empty already. In one brief moment it had become not a home, just a shell.

"Do you remember your golden wedding anniversary party, Dad?"

*

There had been over twenty-five people squashed into the kitchen. Uncle Tom had stood up on the kitchen worktop, doing an impression of some frog he'd seen in his garden. He'd slipped and, being rather drunk, ended up falling into the sink with his bottom firmly wedged in. It had taken four men to get him out and persuade him to stay still on the sofa, where he couldn't come to any further harm. June had tried to sober him up with coffee, but Ted had told her that she was wasting her time.

The party had finished late, but Anna had woken up early the next morning to clean the house.

The party had been well-planned. A date had been marked in the diary, guests had been sent invitations, the wine and beer had been carefully selected and fine platters of food had been lovingly prepared. In the aftermath, hardly any flat surface downstairs was free from an empty bottle, used napkin, dirty plate or glass.

As Anna had walked through the house clearing up, she had recalled distinctive moments from the party. Debris littered each room, yet each item had some special significance. The can of lager, half drunk, was more than just a half empty can of lager. It was the can that Uncle Tom put down precariously behind the sofa in order to do his party trick: his impression of Frank Spencer trying to placate Betty. By putting the can of lager into the bin it somehow took away the memory of his hilarious performance. Dad had drawn in the condensation of the window to keep the score of a game of charades and as Anna took her cloth to the glass, she felt she was erasing the victory of the winners and that all those inspired performances would soon be forgotten.

Anna had done a fine job and when her parents came down it was as though the party had never happened.

*

Anna recognised that same feeling now; she felt the urge to tidy up, to sort through and refresh the house.

"Tom was out of order, it really was outrageous," Ted protested, although smiling, "the sink has never recovered, it still leaks now!"

"I'm just going to get Mum a book to read." Anna's voice echoed along the corridor as she made her way upstairs, "do you know if she's finished everything she's started?" Anna didn't wait for an answer, something was pulling her up the stairs. Her natural curiosity wanted to know what was there, what might need sorting out.

"There might be something in our room," Ted called up, "I know Mary gave us a load of books at Christmas."

Anna had tried to appear nonchalant towards the possibility of her father moving house, but her anxiety was growing as the thought of selling her childhood home became more probable.

"Actually, Anna, I think they're in your room," Ted called up the stairs.

My room, Anna thought. How funny it was to think they still kept a bedroom for her, so many years after leaving home. As she walked through her bedroom doorway the familiar feeling of the room returned. She immediately walked to the window, as she had so often done when entering her room, and gazed down to survey the garden. The room represented the first twenty-three years of her life. Her parents hadn't really done much with the room since she had left. They'd replaced her single bed with a double, but really the décor hadn't changed at all. It was like a second home for her.

"Are you in tonight, Anna?" Her father called up, "I could get some minced beef out of the freezer, or did you want to eat out?"

Anna was gazing at the garden shed as he spoke. The shed where she'd had her first proper kiss. Her father's words invaded her reverie as she remembered the taste of her boyfriend's lips.

"Of course, yeah, that would be nice."

"I'll do a chilli con carne if you like?" Ted replied.

Her boyfriend had only been a year older than her, but at the time that made him seem grown-up and mature. She remembered how she had enjoyed his wonderful mouth and strangely the smell of his sweat, which still to this day she had never told anyone. Ostensibly she had taken him in there to get him to fix the lawnmower, but she had hoped the intimacy of the shed would lead him to steal a kiss. She had enjoyed the success of her plan as much as the sensation of skin-to-skin contact.

"Any luck with the book?" Ted continued to call out, "actually, I think there may be something in Carrie's room."

As she left her room she noted the heights that had been marked off on the door architrave as she had grown up, now quite grubby and illegible. She walked across the landing and into the spare room, which still had her sister's name on the door. When she was sixteen she'd had a boyfriend to stay. He was allowed to stay in Carrie's room as she was away. During the day Anna had visited him there, leaving the door wide open, and enjoying the excitement of being in close proximity to him in a room with a bed. Anna laughed as she remembered her mum and dad patrolling the landing as she went to bed, ensuring there was no detour on her way back from brushing her teeth.

In the room there was now the ugly beige sofa that Mum had decided did not suit the lounge, six weeks after they had bought it. June wasn't wasteful and couldn't bring herself to get rid of it. Above the chest of drawers was a picture, a family portrait of the four of them, painted by her aunt. It was a gift that, although well done, bore no resemblance to any of them. June wouldn't have it downstairs but had always said, "We need it somewhere on display, just in case my sister asks where it is."

"There aren't any books in here, Dad, Mum's had a good clear out." Anna quickly left the room and walked down the stairs.

"Sorry, I know where they are, they've been tidied into the garage." Ted's voice gradually softened as Anna came back in to sight. "I think she's been planning some kind of hideous car boot sale," he grinned.

Anna opened the interconnecting door to the garage. As she stepped inside she felt the coolness of the air, and smelt the musty, oily smells of the car and tools. Glancing up she spotted the broken go-cart hanging on the wall, still waiting to be fixed. This was the room where her father had tried to enthuse her about mechanics, but had failed.

"I've got something!" Anna announced, raising her voice. She put her hand on a collection of English twentieth-century poetry. "It doesn't matter if she's already read this, poetry is poetry. The more you know it, the more you like it; like old friends." With her goal accomplished, Anna skipped out of the garage, chuckling to herself as she remembered her father really had just discussed making a meal with her. Life really was quite bizarre sometimes!

Chapter Two

Ted bent down to kiss June, his lips tickled her cheek. As he stood their eyes met and made their wordless communication.

Ted thought how June looked too well to be in a hospital bed. A fleeting schoolboy thought crossed his mind that he could just pack up her things and all of them could go home. It was all so unreal: the tubes invading her body and the box rhythmically squeaking her pulse; people in uniforms with their name badges; patients sitting around in beds not doing anything.

"What did the doctors say?"

June waited to answer, she waited to find the right words. "I won't be coming home, Ted. You're still going to have to visit me each day please." Ted's mouth opened, he looked away, his frown deepened. "I'm being a right old pain. Sorry. But you really don't need to bring me lunch, dear. The lunches aren't that bad here really, but thank you. Just bring me some special treats," she said as she smiled, hoping to lighten Ted's spirits.

"Do you want me to talk to the doctor, dear?" Ted asked, "shall I get all the details from him?"

"Yes, dear, you do that. He was around just a few minutes ago, he can't have gone far." She reached for his hand. "There is no point in being short with him, darling. There's nothing they could have done." He stood up and sighed heavily. "We just got there too late. We've already had our second opinion."

Ted, needing a moment to gather his thoughts, turned and walked to the bedroom window. He found himself following a couple walking along the path to the maternity wing. They must have been in their early thirties. The woman's stomach was absurdly stretched and misshapen with their baby. The father was walking slightly ahead, leading the woman. Both walked in silence and looked serious, focused on their journey. The man was carrying a large, pink carry sack, holding it slightly ahead of him as though it were a thing he had nothing to do with.

Ted found himself smiling. Seeing the couple took him back to the time when June and he had made a similar journey, to the very same building, for Anna to be delivered. He smiled as he remembered how ill-prepared he had been for the event. Weeks before June had told him not to worry about the due date and that she would have everything arranged. She'd told him to just concentrate on his career. When it came to assisting with the first nappy in the hospital he had made a right prat of himself. His total ineptitude at holding Anna and the nappy at the same time had been laughable. June was not worried about it, after all, she would be doing all the nappy changing in the future. Yet she had been concerned about the amount of attention Ted had received from a couple of nurses who were very willing to help him. She had put an end to that straight away by getting out of bed for the first time and taking over.

June had had everything under control. Her attention to detail was a constant source of success for the young family. Anna and Carrie were raised in a happy and organised home, and to all of them it seemed as though nothing had ever really gone wrong in their lives. Nothing, anyway, that couldn't be overcome. Ted never resented the control June exerted over the family and his life, for it was delivered with love and all was done with the family's best interest at heart. She was a fine mother, and Ted was proud of the daughters that they had raised. Ted would never have put up with this level of control from anyone else. Indeed, at work Ted had been fondly nicknamed 'General Monty' by his colleagues. Although they had often suffered with a larger workload, they had also enjoyed sharing in the successes of his management.

"I'll be going to the hospice tomorrow," June continued, "you know, the one in Lavington. Do you remember when we visited Mary there?"

Ted nodded, he was deciding whether or not he should go after the doctor to learn more about what June was saying. He found it difficult to focus when June spoke of her illness. June was pale and looking thin, he hated to think of her so frail and vulnerable. It seemed so strange to be with her like this, he just wanted her to spring out of bed and take control like she had always done. "Is there anything I can get you..." he stumbled as he searched for a suggestion, "...a cup of tea?"

"Oh yes, that would be lovely," June answered, "could you make it properly, from the kettle I mean. I don't think I can bear anymore from that machine."

"Do we have your sweeteners?" Ted was immediately annoyed with himself for not knowing the answer.

"They're in my handbag. Anna, come and sit next to me. Show me the pictures of your holiday on your phone," she said, patting the seat next to her.

Anna sat down and busied herself with finding the pictures. While they were driving over to the hospital she had practiced the things that she wanted to say. She was determined to be more careful than when she had spoken with Dad. She knew that what she had said about him moving house had been too direct by the way that he had not wanted to answer her. This visit to see her mum seemed so important, so vital. Her mother was dying. The time that they could share together was finite. These were precious moments. She didn't want to create any awkward situations by saying the wrong thing.

"The holiday seems like a lifetime away," Anna explained, "mind you, saying that, we are still unpacking."

June welcomed the opportunity to smile. "Has it changed?" June asked, "the hotel I mean. Is that wacky waiter still there?"

"Yes, and even wackier! He was wearing one of those spinning bowties."

They both laughed.

Now that she was sitting next to her mum, she didn't really feel like saying the things that she had carefully prepared. Those important matters to be discussed now seemed banal and inconsequential. Before she arrived there seemed to be a hundred and one things to deliberate: unspoken words that need to be said; clutter that wanted clearing; unsettled matters to be resolved; confusion that should be clarified; and solutions for problems in which procrastination had reigned for too long. However, the opportunities to do so were slipping away. Anna struggled to organise her thoughts.

"Stupid phone, I know they're here somewhere. I think the phone's put them out of order."

Slowly she resigned herself to the status quo. The things that had been unsaid for years were probably already known. Her mother and father were good at that, knowing what she was worried about before she had even realised that she was actually worrying. She hated it when they did that. Their apparent mastery of situations in which she was so uncertain made her feel quite incompetent. Perhaps it was wrong to bring up all those unresolved issues, they belonged to a different time and to bring them up now would be out of context.

"Anna?" June said, "I want you to do something for me."

"Yes, Mum?" Anna looked up.

"I want you to take my thimble collection to the Oxfam shop in Chichester."

"But, Mum!" Anna protested.

"No, Anna, it's OK. No one really wants it and they'll know how to get the best out of it there, it's for a good cause too. It was fun collecting it in the beginning, but you know, after a while it just got in the way. I spent more time cleaning it than I did looking at it."

Anna didn't protest anymore.

"Ted, be sure to take out our thimble before it goes, you can keep that safe for me. But my mum's thimble, that will go with me please, you know, in a pocket or something." She waited for him to turn towards her, "Always with love, darling."

"Yes. Always with love."

Chapter Three

"It was such a good send-off, Anna, thank you," her father praised, "I just didn't have the energy to put it all together."

"I'm glad you're glad. The things that you said in the church were beautiful. I've never heard you speak like that before, about Mum, about your life before…"

"B.C.," Ted interjected, "before children!" he laughed.

As Anna watched her father, it struck her that he appeared quite different. Was it his clothes or was it just the way he carried himself? In fact, the whole morning had been quite contrary to her expectation.

She had wanted to visit him, as it had been a couple of weeks since they had last spoken. It had seemed strange, coming to the house knowing that her mother wouldn't be there. Just like it had been strange after leaving home, when she had stopped using her key and had instead knocked on the door and waited for her parents to answer. But this morning Anna was greeted with an entirely different welcome. Dad had kissed her on the cheek, followed by another kiss on the other cheek. He'd never done that before.

As they sat on the patio, soaking up the morning sunshine, she welcomed the peace and pace of the conversation; it seemed almost medicinal. It wasn't a chatty and vibrant conversation, like the ones that she'd had with her mother, it was more measured, yet it felt good. Apple and cherry blossom provided a technicolour highlight for the manicured flower borders and lawn. Their relaxation seemed even more motionless as they watched the birds feverishly flying to and fro, busy with their spring agenda and joyful with the warmer weather.

When Anna had arrived Ted had spotted the 'on duty eyes' of his daughter, she was there to make sure he was alright. But he had seen something else. Anna was quiet; she was not her usual talkative self.

"I've been looking at quite a few places," he said. Anna looked up, trying hard to appear relaxed. "There's a little flat down by the canal that would suit me, I think. I always hankered as a boy to live in a houseboat, this seems like the next best thing. I'll try and arrange a second viewing. You could come too and give me a woman's perspective."

As he spoke Anna noticed that he was fiddling with something in his pocket.

"Ooh! I'd love that, Dad. Any time! That sounds like great fun." Anna was smiling at the suggestion, it was the sort of thing she would have done with her mother.

"Thank you for the offer of moving in," Ted continued, "it's nice to have that to fall back on to, but it would make things quite cramped for you."

"I could always get somewhere bigger..." Anna stopped herself, she had heard the pleading tone in her voice.

As Ted poured the coffee from the *cafetière* a plane flew overhead and disturbed the silence. It soon passed and the garden returned to its dreamy tranquillity. Anna noted the posh biscuits that had been laid out neatly on a plate, the sugar bowl with its silver spoon and the bone china teacups. Was this the first time Dad had ever made her coffee? She had anticipated an old mug and a packet of digestives. The silence continued, and neither Anna nor Ted felt the need to fill it with aimless chatter.

"You know your mother was singularly the best thing that ever happened to me. She really was so wonderful." Ted eventually spoke, looking towards the back of the garden as though he were watching June planting out in the flowerbed. "I know that some other people have amazing and passionate loves, or love affairs in exotic places," he laughed, "some couples have a relationship based on steamy sex, or engaging and interesting intellectual conversation." He raised an eyebrow, "I think June's love was the best for me, it was a one-off."

Anna was intrigued as she watched her father concentrate on his words whilst he stared in the direction of the old oak tree.

"I guess everyone's experience of love is pretty much different. Somehow, I feel like I didn't give as much as I got..." he paused briefly as he turned to Anna. "I sometimes wake up at night and worry that perhaps June didn't know how much I appreciated her."

Anna admired how her father was able to speak about her mother with calmness and clarity; something she felt was quite difficult to do when she spoke with her husband, David. Dad seemed to understand something that she had been looking for but was unable to grasp. He was speaking with an acceptance, the acceptance that she needed. But she could also hear that he wanted her to take in what he had to say. Was this one of his planned conversations?

Even if it was, Anna loved the closeness of this moment, hoping that it would be a more permanent fixture in their relationship. They had always been a force to be reckoned with, Mum and Dad, always agreeing and showing solidarity. Perhaps now her father would look for that with her.

Again though, she noticed him fiddling in his trousers. *Oh God*, she thought, *I really must say something about that. It's turning into quite a new habit. It's the sort of thing Mum would sort out straight away.*

"I know you'd like me to move in, Anna. You'd like to look after me and make sure I'm OK..." he paused, waiting for Anna to look up, "but you see, it's time I did that for myself. Look after myself I mean. I need to do a few things on my own."

Ted smiled, hoping Anna would smile back. "Don't look so disappointed, Anna. You've got your family. I don't think your husband would be too impressed having some old fogey around all the time, cramping his style."

"David would be fine with it, Dad. Anyway, what about cooking, how are you going to do that? You've never even boiled an egg in your life!"

Ted let Anna's light-hearted protest resonate before he responded.

"Well, I think that's the whole point. It's about time I did. Anyway, I've always got the ladies down at the golf club, they're queuing up to have me around for a meal!"

In that moment Anna realised her father was going to be alright. Even though she was starting to feel closer to her father she still felt the resistance of their relationship; she would always be the daughter, he would always be the father.

"They're all falling over themselves to look after me, and perhaps I might let them," he winked at Anna, "but not before I've looked after myself," he said resolutely.

"OK, Dad, I get it, I was just worried, now that Mum has gone, now that we've lost her."

"No, not lost," Ted said softly, "June will always be with me... with us both," he corrected himself. "June is with us in so many ways." As he said this he took out from his pocket the object that he had been fiddling with. Anna saw it was the thimble. The silver thimble that Dad had given Mum on their engagement. Absentmindedly he proceeded to try to put the thimble on his different fingers until it found his little finger, the only one it fitted. He took it off and repeated his little ritual, trying again to find the best fit.

"June will always be with us. She's in everything we do..." he paused, "...you're so like her! Some of the things you do make me laugh. It's as if you were mimicking her. Look how you're holding your coffee cup, it's just like June does. Look at your daughters. Every time Emily smiles I see June. I see her like she was on the first day we met. I think Emily may have even bought the same dresses that June wore in the sixties," he smiled, "funny how the styles come back."

Wood pigeons cooed somewhere high up in the tree above them, while a sparrow flew down to the patio and started his delicate song. The morning breeze had disappeared, leaving the garden still and, with the last of the clouds disappearing, it felt like the first day of summer.

"June would have loved the garden today," Ted said wistfully. Anna didn't know what to say, it was such a sad and yet joyful statement, all in one sentence. "More coffee?" Ted asked as he stood and collected her cup. Carefully he took the thimble off his little finger and placed it next to his glasses.

As her father walked back to the kitchen Anna sat in silence, taking in the serenity of the garden. She let her mind wander, not thinking of anything in particular. She saw the thimble on the table and considered whether she had ever picked it up before. She knew how special it was to him and appreciated that it was a lot more practical as a keepsake than a house! She reached out to hold it, looking up to see if her father was coming. Now that it was out of the display cabinet it seemed like more of a private object, like holding her mum's diary.

She felt the little ridge along its bottom and it sparkled silver in the sunlight. It reflected light across her eyes as she created a circular motion with it between her thumb and index finger. She then caught it at such an angle that she noticed for the first time an inscription engraved along the base; '*Love begets love*'.

She smiled, excited at her discovery, as she looked closely at the italic writing. She wanted to talk to her father about his choice of words. *Love comes from love, is that what it means?* she wondered. How had he gone about getting the thimble engraved and how had her mum reacted when she saw it? Was it indeed Mum or Dad that had engraved the thimble? Anna was remembering now. Her mother had routinely polished the thimble and she'd always thought it strange, given that the thimble would never get dirty inside the cabinet. Why hadn't she looked at it before?

As she heard her father walking back from the kitchen she contemplated the remainder of the afternoon. She felt a sudden urge to get back and see David and the kids. It would be nice to get around the table and enjoy a Sunday roast tonight. They could all relax before the busy week ahead.

Anna stood up as her father approached. "Dad, I've got a hundred and one questions about this thimble!" Ted looked up from the tray, concerned both about what the questions might be and that he had left the thimble behind. "I love the inscription," Anna continued, "I want you to tell me all about it, but not now, I've got to get back."

"But what about your coffee!?" Ted questioned.

"Sorry, Dad, I just feel like I should get back and see David and the girls. I'll call up in the week and we'll arrange for you to come over and have a meal, you can tell me all about it then. If you can fit us in that is, between all the girls at the golf club," she grinned.

"That sounds like a lovely idea," Ted said, smiling, and as Anna stepped forward he wrapped his arms around her. "So good to see you!" It had been a long time since he had given her one of his lovely big bear hugs, just like she would always receive as a child.

Anna felt the warmth of her father against her. He was a lot taller than her and that seemed to amplify the paternal quality of their embrace. It was funny to think that they hadn't done that at the funeral and now it seemed to bring on the same raft of emotions that she had allowed herself to feel briefly on the day. She felt the anger; her mum had been taken from her!

Anna had gone to the funeral without a handkerchief. She had decided that she would do her crying later in private. But when it came to it, her feelings were too strong, and keeping them contained behind a dam had paralysed her with the fear of acknowledging them. When she did eventually test her strength they had released themselves with such vigour that they gushed out like a tsunami, crushing and sweeping her off her feet. As everyone had stood up at the pews she had no choice but to stay seated and try her best to mop her tears; tears that shook her to her core, leaving her body uncontrollably. She remembered the face of her husband, as he looked at her with a complete lack of comprehension of her pain, as well as fear that he was unable to help her. The force of her feelings had been a shock to her. Her mother had taught her to be strong. It might have been the first time in her life that she had actually considered man's ultimate end, man's mortality, the nature of that finality and its inevitability.

"Yes, Dad, it was lovely to see you too. I'm so pleased you're..." She didn't finish her sentence. Her father squeezed her harder and Anna felt her independence and her calm demeanour begin to slip away. She felt for a brief moment unsteady on her feet and that in some way her father was holding her up. Her father was old but strong. Anna tried to stop thinking of her mother, she didn't want to lose the peace she had found sitting in the garden. She made a firm decision to switch off her thoughts. She managed once again to push her loss right back down to a dark and unused part of her mind. Anna stiffened and stood up straighter, separating them.

"Was it Mum's inscription, Dad? The idea of it I mean," Anna continued, not waiting for an answer, "does it mean if you give love then you'll get it back?"

"Kind of, but not like if you fall in love with someone they'll fall in love with you back," Ted chuckled, "that would be too easy." He smiled, but Anna had her serious expression on. Ted realised that Anna would need a full answer, yet it felt disloyal to talk about and release something that he and June had shared together.

"Was it something Mum had wanted, to put that on the thimble. You didn't buy it like that, did you?"

"Well guessed, Anna," he smiled. "Your mother had it put on when we got back from Venice. It took me a bit of time to realise what it meant to her, what the words meant to her, I mean. It was to do with her childhood." Ted looked at Anna. She was erect and faced him straight on, her arms by her sides, and completely attentive to every word. Anna listened to find meaning, hoping to understand the forces that had guided her childhood. "We're going back to the war, when your mum was an evacuee. You know, when they took all the kids out of London during the bombing. Your granddad was sent for service up in Norfolk and your nan was busy keeping things together with two jobs."

Anna looked at her dad and sensed that he was holding something back. She thought of the old sepia pictures in the family album. "Mum was unhappy? Did she suffer?"

Ted hesitated, was this what Anna needed to hear? She already felt the pain of her loss. He slowly sat down again. "Everything changed, I can remember it myself, those early days of the war. Yes, it was exciting for some, and for others it was almost a release, it had been coming for such a long time. It almost felt inevitable. But for your mum, her whole life fell apart. She lost your Uncle Phillip in France, quite soon after it started. She didn't get on with the folks in her new home, they had children, but they were quite a bit older. Your mum would have only been eight. There wasn't much time for Nan to write to your mum either."

"I didn't realise she was so young!"

"Those years were great for me, my brother and I loved it, making bomb shelters; playing war games; spotting and naming the planes; listening to our progress on the radio. But it wasn't so great for your mum. Uncle Tom came back from Norfolk after a few weeks, but she stayed down there for pretty much the whole of the war. Her host family were quite poor and they had her working on the allotment and doing all the sewing. People used to alter and repair clothes then.

Clothes were passed down between family members. They might reuse the material more than just once. Anyway, there wasn't much fun to be had. Everything was in short supply and although she had her own ration book, she didn't think she got all her food. One of the winters was really bitter and she'd caught flu and nearly died. She remembers just before the following winter an old woman she hardly knew knitted her some bed socks. They made the icy nights bearable. She was baffled though at the time, trying to work out the reason for the woman's kindness, in fact she was so taken aback that she'd forgotten to say thank you."

Anna had known that her mum had been an evacuee, but her unhappiness was a revelation. She had assumed that it had been an adventure for her. She remembered her mum had said that those years had been a real education and that she had really matured during that time. Anna now understood what she meant: she'd learnt some tough lessons. So perhaps her mum had spent the rest of her life making a world where love was at the centre of everything she did. She gave love not to receive it, not because she expected it back and not to keep her husband close, but because for her love was life's meaning, its purpose. "So the inscription, it was a promise! A promise to herself?"

"Yes! She wanted things to be different for you and Carrie."

Anna had stayed on her feet as she listened to her father. She walked closer to her chair but quickly stopped herself. Out of nowhere a new question arose, *did David know how much she loved him?* "I feel like I've got to get back, Dad, but I'd love to hear more about it all when I see you next."

They walked to the front door in silence. Anna was deep in thought and Ted was also pensive, having remembered his wife's troubled past as well as feeling Anna was leaving earlier than expected.

As Ted slowly opened the front door he stepped out and surveyed the street, taking in the air of the afternoon. Anna hesitated to step through and instead she looked at her father's arms. Ted instinctively reached out for her and hugged her once more. As he held her she couldn't stop thinking about her mum, so young, so far away from her family and so unhappy. Was love rationed too?

This time it was Ted that pulled away, yet he kept hold of Anna's arms. He looked her in the eyes and then put the back of his hand gently to her cheek. "It will get easier you know, just give it time." And then Anna felt something being put into her hand. "It's time for you to have it, now you know why it's so special."

Anna reached for her father and pulled him back in. There was no use in pretending; she couldn't keep anything from him. Inside she laughed at herself. She had left the house that morning on a duty call to cheer up her father and had instead found something between them that was new. She was looking forward to getting to know her father. She was slowly forming a new understanding, a new way of feeling about the loss of her mother.

Luke McEwen

His and Hers Lists

All married couples should learn the art of battle as they should learn the art of making love. Good battle is objective and honest - never vicious or cruel. Good battle is healthy and constructive, and brings to a marriage the principle of equal partnership.

- Andre Maurois, 1885 – 1967

Chapter One

As he watched the traffic lights stay red, his phone chimed a reminder of today's meeting. His mind immediately focused on his goal. He just wanted the best for his family and that included a good relationship with all of them: his wife and his children. *How can I do that?* The lights would soon change. He advanced the accelerator in anticipation, throwing the car into first and keeping his foot on the clutch.

The sound of the car's indicator came into sharp focus, the tick-tock echoing his heartbeat. And then the sound was lost to him, vanishing as he thought of the dinner table last night, where no one had had anything to say. They just weren't getting on like they should. He needed a new campaign, a new mission to get them to where they should be. More fun, smiles and laughter, just like the old days. After all, that was why he put in the long hours at the office.

On his steering wheel he hit voice activation. "Call office," he said, clearly and precisely. The call tone came through the car speakers.

"Good morning, Mark Farley's office; how may I help you?"

"Good morning, Janice, how are you? Good weekend?"

The lights turned green. Mark released his left foot and sped his Audi across the junction.

"I'm fine, thanks, I had a lovely weekend. Tim and I…"

"Sorry to interrupt, Janice, but there are a couple of things that need doing." Mark glanced into his rear view mirror to check he could turn, then flicked the indicator.

"That's fine, Mark, no worries. Shoot!"

"Can you send me a PDF of that new company resolution? I'll collect it on my phone."

"Will do."

Mark waited for the oncoming traffic to clear, tutting at its slowness.

"I have a meeting with Annabel this morning. No doubt our Christmas plans will be discussed. Can you remind me if I have booked any holiday in December?"

He turned the car right with one hand as he used the other to turn up the volume.

"Sorry, Mark, you cut out there. Can you repeat?"

He approached a queue of traffic, which was waiting for the car park. "Damn!" he muttered. "Sorry, Janice, not damning you, just this bloody traffic..." He hesitated, trying to work out what information he needed. He crept forward, keeping his front bumper inches from the car in front, ignoring the yellow hash lines.

"Let me know my diary dates for December, will you? What holiday is booked out. Can you let me have that by text? I'll need it in a few minutes. Also, did the Rackham proposal come in this morning?"

Mark was being beeped. He had blocked the traffic. He put his hand up to apologise and gave a half-hearted smile. "Janice, I'll talk to you later. I've got to get parked up. Bye for now." Mark hung up; he didn't wait for Janice to respond.

*

Annabel sat there like a queen, dressed in all her finery. Her pose was firm, each limb held like a well-positioned angle lamp, and with it she focused her attention on him. Mark remembered the stain on his tie that he hadn't got around to removing yet. *And look at the state of my fingernails!* he thought. He realised that he was sitting awkwardly on his chair, all buckled over on the edge. He found it difficult to lift his head and meet her eyes.

He had known that home wasn't the right place for this conversation, but now that they were at the busy coffee bar, this wasn't quite right either. It wasn't like work, where he could call a member of staff to a meeting room. With annual appraisals the member of staff was in the correct frame of mind for him: hopeful for praise, but aware (and agonising) that they might receive criticism. The meeting room was his territory, allowing the inequality of the manager-junior relationship to thrive.

But the coffee bar was his wife's domain, where she held court. She was at ease with the strongly coloured walls, Sorento lemon, Rothko red, pictures that seemed to lack recognisable object and with supposed profundities written across the wall.

Mark drew a long breath and looked for the right place to start. "Darling." *Yes*, he thought, *a good start.* "I wanted to meet today to..." He hesitated.

Annabel, still focused on her husband like a laser beam, dived in. "Yes, darling, so nice that we could meet this morning. I was a little worried that I wasn't going to have time, since the ladies are having a morning session at the club."

Mark watched her mouth as she spoke. For the first time, he noticed that her canines were actually quite large. As she said the word 'tennis', her mouth opened wider and revealed them further. He found himself holding back the idea that she was an Alsatian, just about to bark – or indeed, bite.

"It's been so difficult to get out and play this summer," Annabel continued, "what with all the rain and the club house being refurbished. It's been a real pain." Annabel stared at Mark as she stirred her coffee. Without breaking her gaze she fingered her caramel waffle and then broke a piece off to squeeze between her teeth.

There was a pause. Mark was struggling to focus. He knew that this was going to be difficult; he also knew that he had to make a start. If he could just begin, then surely it would soon start to flow; not dissimilar to an interview. He simply had to make the candidate feel at ease, and then the conversation could run smoothly, back and forth. But he couldn't think of anything.

Annabel served up a new topic. "Mark, I really need us to look at our Christmas plans for this year. We must choose some dates. You know how things get booked up so quickly this time of year."

"Darling, of course; but I really wanted to meet today so that we could…" He paused, and as he struggled to find his words he noticed that Annabel was about to interrupt again. *Damn it!* he thought. He should have planned this better.

"Excuse me, is this chair free?" A teenager stood at their table with one hand on the chair next to them. Mark glanced up and, without making eye contact, gave a nod. He looked back to Annabel and smiled, but she did not reciprocate. Mark was, however, suddenly comforted: he had remembered his list. The list that would give him the perfect place to start.

Mark had begun the list five months before. He acknowledged that it had been a long time coming. It had been remiss of him not to have raised the issues earlier. That was the whole point of appraisals: they gave the opportunity for a 'frank exchange of views', to 'clear the air', to 'make new resolutions' and 'allow constructive development'. Most importantly, it allowed people to 'grow and knit their aspirations more closely with the company's'.

The first few items were just general housekeeping. In very much the same way that he ensured the office was kept clean, he felt that home should be tidy too. At work, files should not be left on desks, and paperwork needed to end up in the right place, even if that was the bin. At home, plates should end up in the dishwasher when the meal was complete. And a cleaning schedule would be good. That would avoid the embarrassment they had last year, when his mother had turned up for a surprise visit and had seen the rubbish bags waiting to go out, mixed up with the booty of Annabel's last shopping expedition. Mark started his list with, 'Cleaning and tidying required'.

Then there was spending. Just as at work, a budget was required: nothing too formal, but a general regard to ensure that outgoings were not larger than incomings. It kept the business on track, and he thought it also necessary for their joint account. Why did it slip in and out of overdraft? Mark added 'Basic control over spending' to his list.

Next, he felt that Annabel had put on quite a bit of weight in the last five years, and he was concerned it was bad for her health. There were lots of programmes on TV about this, and how it affected one's motivation, sex drive, longevity and confidence. Mark was always very proud of the pastoral care he gave to the young intakes at the company. One didn't have to say much; just the right words at the right time would have the desired effect. Mark wrote down, 'Weight gain'.

But there were more pressing matters for the list. There had been some events lately that had "compromised his relationship" with Annabel, and it would be good to seek an explanation.

For example, at the dinner party with Ben and Sheila, why hadn't she backed him up in his argument about the Prime Minister? In their twenties, they were a force to be reckoned with on the dinner party circuit. Annabel would up the ante with a sweeping remark, and when she was challenged, Mark would come in with the latest facts to support her. Then Annabel would give a defining conclusion. They were known as the Debating Team. So what happened last weekend? Annabel had left him floundering to finish his argument and Ben came in for an easy win. Mark added, 'Team player: I can't do it all on my own'.

Also, why had she not supported him in his discipline of the children? At nineteen Tim was at a difficult age. One had to influence rather than order, gently offer different approaches, and recommend, not command. When Tim had taken the car without asking, driven it to a music festival and returned it muddy inside and out and minus a tank of petrol, Mark had drawn the line and requested that Tim make good. He was initially pleased to find that the car was both filled with petrol and clean. Subsequently, however, it transpired that Annabel had given Tim the money for both the petrol and a professional valet. Mark added 'Parenting skills tune-up?'

Sex. Mark felt that sex should happen more often that it did. He had read in *Cosmopolitan* that in order to keep your man you should put 'Sex' high on the agenda. Proficient women who wanted to keep their marriage healthy put sex on the 'To do' list at least twice a week. Mark thought that would be sufficient. He was confused as to why their sex life had dissipated to less than once a month. He was pretty sure that he had maintained his standards and his attention to detail. He was still doing it the way he always had. He wrote, 'More sex'.

Time apart. Annabel was always very busy. She had her bridge evening, the book club, three games of tennis a week, WI and NADFAS, her coffee mornings, and then, of course, the cocktail parties. Mark felt that Annabel needed to be a little more grounded. Her time with all these things was a tremendous distraction from getting back into some sort of paid work, and he saw so little of her. He remembered the days when she would accompany him to the classic car meetings, and when she would come and see him play squash. Things were better then: they were more in tune with each other. So the next item was, 'Togetherness'.

Toxic friendship. He had read in his *Management Today* magazine that one should vet the people that come into contact with your employees. There were certain relationships that caused ill feeling and a loss of focus. It was important to identify these people early and remove them as best as one could. Mark felt very much this way in regard to Annabel's tennis coach. It had been an awkward first meeting. Mark had gone to pick Annabel up from the tennis club, but hadn't realised that she was having a private lesson. He had gone to the side of the court and tried to catch Annabel's attention, but they were engrossed in their game. As they finished Mark tried to introduce himself but the coach avoided eye contact.

There was also the time when they'd been out shopping and had bumped into him in the street. He had only talked to Annabel and not to Mark, ignoring all his attempts at the usual pleasantries. Mark added 'Tennis coach to go; not our sort'.

Irritating habits. Mark knew that he had some of these since Annabel would point them out to him, but whilst he was in the flow of writing his list he thought he might as well add some of Annabel's. Probably the most irritating was her 'shop and bag drop' habit. Annabel would spend the day shopping, collecting a plethora of bags, and then get back just before she had to get ready to go out again. Consequently she would leave all the bags on the kitchen table or the lounge floor, entirely unopened. There they would stay for days, becoming an obstacle course. You could tell that Annabel found this all very exciting, for by the time she unpacked the bags she had forgotten what she had bought. And often, when she decided that she needed to take something back, it was too long after the purchase or the receipt was lost. Mark added, 'Shopping bag chaos'.

The mother-in-law. They tended to see Annabel's mother and not his. In a way this was understandable, for Mark's mother was somewhat overbearing and had never fully accepted that any of Mark's girlfriends were good enough for him. Yet perhaps Annabel could make things easier for him? She was good with people and when she was with his mother her company made things run smoothly. He did the same for Annabel, after all. The atmosphere was always more convivial when they both visited her mother, he made sure of that. Mark finished with, 'More visits to my mother'.

So, in the end Mark's list looked like this:

Cleaning and tidying required
Basic control over spending
Weight gain
Team player; I can't do this on my own
Parenting skills tune-up?
More sex
Togetherness
Tennis coach to go; not our sort
Shopping bag chaos
More visits to my mother

He discreetly got out the list. A quick refresher of the main points would give him what he needed. He scanned it quickly, and made the decision to start on the fourth point, since it was the least sensitive.

"Darling, I wanted to talk about –"

"Can I clear your table, sir?" A young man was standing over him, awkwardly waiting for an answer.

"Yes, of course." Mark tried to maintain focus on his presentation.

"Mark." Too late! Annabel was in. "Flights for the Caribbean always get booked early. We need to get something in the diary with the children, and then we can get our tickets booked. I'd like very much to go back to the same place; you know, the hotel with the funny infinity pool. Now, do you have your diary with you, darling? If you haven't, I'm going to throw some dates at you and you'll have to get back to me."

Mark sighed. They had already finished their lattes and muffins, and he hadn't even started the first point on the agenda. This was hopeless. He needed to make a proper start or postpone the meeting.

For the first time Mark noticed the toilet door was open. *Ah ha*, he thought, *the toilet trick!*

"Darling, do you mind if I go to the loo? Just give me a few minutes." Mark stood up and felt awkward that he had asked permission to go to the loo and agreed an amount of time to complete the activity. Though he couldn't help wondering if he had asked for enough time.

Once there, Mark took a long, deep breath, straightened his tie and retied his shoelaces. Turning to the mirror, he gave himself a long stare. He looked deep into his eyes and waited for his friendly face to smile back. He noticed that his hair needed a trim, and his eyebrows too. What on earth had happened there? Perhaps he should investigate some male grooming techniques. His shirt had seen better days; the collar had refused to iron flat and looked the wrong shade of white. It was time to spruce up a bit. *You can't go into a meeting and not present yourself at your best; schoolboy error!* With that, he smiled. The friendly face returned, and Mark felt soothed. He gave a little laugh. OK, so he had failed in his preparation for the meeting, but it was never too late to start again.

Perhaps the whole idea of the list was wrong anyway. It was meant to bolster his confidence, but actually it would only lead to a conflict. He couldn't see Annabel calmly going through his points and seeking a resolution. Most likely she would immediately take a defensive position and go on the attack. Her debating skills would take over and their positions would only become more entrenched. No, the plan needed to be more subtle. Over the coming months, he would hint at a few issues. Perhaps at Christmas he'd have more time with Annabel. He could pick off one point at a time.

Mark didn't actually go to the loo, but he rinsed his hands anyway. He wouldn't want Annabel to think he hadn't washed them.

Resigned to his own reticence, he stepped out of the loo. He would talk about Christmas instead, as Annabel had wanted. He had stored up his objections for months, perhaps years, so a couple more months wouldn't make a difference.

He carefully closed the door behind him then walked back into the busy, loud coffee bar. As he approached the table he met Annabel's eyes. They were angry and her face was white. Her pose had collapsed somewhat, yet it still appeared rigid and unyielding. She held something tightly in both hands. Something paper; black handwriting on lined A4.

Mark froze. It was his list. The list he had stupidly left on the table.

He was fully ten feet away from Annabel, but he felt the energy of her rage. She stood up tall, and straightened herself like the string of a longbow being pulled tight and soon to be released. Mark waited for the impact.

She bared her teeth and barked, "How dare you! This is a load of rubbish. Complete and ridiculous nonsense!"

Annabel was suddenly quiet as she eyed him up and down. She glanced back at the list before letting it drop to the table. Her lips disappeared as she pressed them hard together. "Indeed it is so outrageously incorrect, I don't even need to defend myself."

With that, she adjusted her skirt, smoothed her hair and collected her handbag. "Goodbye, Mark," she said firmly, looking at him as though he were an incompetent tradesmen. "We'll let the solicitors sort this out."

She walked away from him and out of the coffee shop, never once looking back. It seemed as if the coffee shop had come to a standstill. Even the barista was staring at him, judging him. The judgement wouldn't be good. *What did you do to upset her?*

What had happened!? His objectives had been completely missed and his strategy had backfired. Did he get it wrong? Yes, he certainly did get it wrong. But the question was *how* wrong. He needed some time to work out what Annabel's reaction meant.

He walked back to the car in silence, trying to piece together the conversation. He wondered what Annabel was doing now. Would she just go straight to the tennis club and take it all out on some balls? What *should* he have said?

Then, suddenly, he was tired of assessing it all. He enjoyed the momentum of just walking, simply putting one foot in front of the other.

After a while he found that he had taken a wrong turn, and it would take an extra few minutes to return to his car. He stopped and breathed in the warm summer air. The sun was shining, and he noticed children laughing in the park. Motionless, he observed them playing. It was the first time that day that he had been still.

Mark smiled. Yes, the meeting really had been badly planned, and his mental rehearsal way off target. But he had got his message across. Annabel had found out what he really thought, without him diluting the strength of his feelings or apologising for his opinions. In fact, the meeting had been outrageously successful. He found himself laughing out loud, and he looked around to see if anyone was watching. As he continued along the pavement he felt a little spring return to his step.

Somewhere at the back of his mind he knew he had a few emails to answer, some phone calls to make and perhaps a meeting that afternoon. But for now they could all wait. The sun was just too good to rush away from.

Chapter Two

Annabel was power walking. Her eyes were fixed on the pavement ahead, and her heart and mind were racing. Even before the meeting, her morning had not started well: she had been told that she was not able to play in a tennis tournament since she had not applied early enough. But then, to be faced with a character assassination from her husband, after giving up a game of tennis to meet him, had left her volcanic with anger, with fists clenched and her lips pressed to whiteness.

Her quick march had taken her some four hundred yards away from the coffee bar, when she abruptly stopped and stood still. She pulled out her mobile, her rage making it difficult to concentrate, and called her friend's number.

"Marge!"

"Annabel? What's wrong?"

"He's gone too far this time, Marge, he's really pissed me off. I just can't believe it. Of all the ingratitude! He actually had it all written down," Annabel spat, "like some kind of agenda! All the things I have…. he thinks I've done!"

"The little shrew!"

Annabel drew her breath. "Just think of everything I've given up for him. I could have been a solicitor! With my own practice!"

"Well, darling, this isn't the first time, is it?"

Was Marge about to say 'I told you so'?

"Look, I know exactly what you're going through – you know all about my saga. I can recommend my legal eagle at the drop of a hat. If you want Carole's number I'll text it to you *right* now!"

Annabel paused. Her mind was still spinning from the moment she had seen 'Tennis coach to go; not our sort' on the list. And the other one: 'Cleaning and tidying required'!

"Yes, do that please, Marge. I just can't believe what I've given up. It's like I've been living in some kind of daydream. No, make that a nightmare!"

"Poor you, sweetie, you just don't deserve it! I wonder why he's suddenly brought it all up now. Is it a bit quiet in the bedroom?"

"Arggh! Boring husband, boring sex. There are two main positions and he alternates them regimentally!"

"Well, *gosh*, Annabel darling, he is such a monster! I always knew he'd let you down. I *will* text you my solicitor's phone number. She's such a good girl; she got me the house, the children and a useful monthly payment." She giggled. "Poor old Harold didn't know what hit him!"

"OK, Marge, I'll let you know how I get on. See you at the club tomorrow."

"Bye, sweetie, take care. Don't worry, dear, there's always sunshine after the rain."

Annabel realised she had been standing in the middle of the pavement holding up the passersby. She moved to the side and waited for Marge's text. She felt calmer now, and more determined. She didn't have to do this alone.

She thought of all the injustices she had suffered. It was she who had kept their kids on side, by persuading them to treat their father with respect; they would otherwise have gone long ago. So many times she had had to explain his behaviour to them. All his drive and inspiration had been eaten up at the office. She could have had a successful career, but he had persuaded her to stay at home and look after the kids. So many years wasted. So many years of her life had gone by, waiting for him to be like his old self. It wasn't a bad lifestyle: the shopping and holidays went some way to make up for not having had the life she really wanted. But now that the kids were leaving the nest, her marriage was a farce. As time went by they had talked less and less; now they hardly spoke at all. None of the unguarded, searching and easy conversations they used to have, peppered with laughter.

Why did he have to control everything in such obsessive detail? It seemed he'd lost the art of just letting go. She caught him once counting the number of loo rolls that had been used. He questioned the children on their methodology and whether some efficiency could be put in place to use less paper.

Did she ever really love him?

Her friends would laugh at him behind his back. She remembered the gardener who had mocked him openly with sarcasm, yet he didn't realise. After he had spoken to the gardener as though he were a servant, the man nicknamed Mark 'Lord of the Manor'. He'd asked the gardener to take special care of the roses he'd planted, and the man had responded by surreptitiously peeing on them.

Actually, she realised, that was how Mark also spoke to her: like a servant. She recalled times when she had been shown how to reconcile her bank account, like some naughty teenager.

Was her reaction to his list so explosive because she was looking for an excuse to end the marriage?

She hadn't wanted to do that herself. She had said 'no' to her tennis coach, Zack.

But now, there were no holds barred. *I could call Zack*, she thought. Thinking about him made her even more agitated. She had refused him. He'd asked her to see him at his home for a private lesson. She knew exactly what had been implied and had declined, out of her depth and feeling some kind of loyalty, not to Mark, but to the idea of marriage and to her family.

"Is it too late?" she said aloud.

She thought back to Zack's texts – how it started. They were guarded yet suggestive; cheeky and saucy, but never direct, in case someone else read them. She thought they were just a bit of fun, but they let her know that he wanted her. She found the exchange not only titillating but absorbing; she loved to receive his texts. In the end, she had texted him back.

So, just as she had done so many times before, she picked up her phone and texted: 'It's happened! Mark has pissed me off completely, the last straw x'

Zack's response was almost instant.

'Where are you? x'

'Park Road x'

'Meet me :) x'

Annabel read the text, and then read the whole text exchange, including yesterday's. What was she hesitating for?

Her phone chimed.

'It's time for me to show you a different kind of technique x'

It was cheesy but it made Annabel feel sexy and excited. *This is really going to happen*, she thought. *Oh God, my life has been on the pause button for too long!*

Her mobile gave another little chime, but this time the text was from Marge. It was the telephone number for the solicitor.

She texted Zack: 'Give me 20, I've got to make a phone call x'

Her fingers found Marge's text and she pressed on the number.

"Smythe and Simpson, how may I direct your call?"

"I'd like to speak to Mrs Smythe, please. Marge Embers recommended her to me."

"Please hold."

Annabel waited.

"Carole Smythe speaking." The lawyer's voice was somewhat curt.

"Hello: my name is Annabel Farley. Marge Embers recommended you to me. I have a ....."

"Ah yes, Marge called me and said you might phone. Can I suggest we put something in the diary?"

Annabel was taken aback. She hadn't expected Marge to have called the solicitor. It was efficient of her but a little presumptuous. She didn't feel ready for a meeting. "For now, can you just give me a little advice?"

"Sure!"

"What should I be doing now? The situation is quite intolerable! I had a bit of shock this morning: my husband..." Annabel paused, waiting for the right words. "My husband attacked me with a list, a self-absorbed rant. I just need something to change. Should I be going to a marriage counsellor or something?"

Mrs Smythe hesitated. "Well do you want more of the same, or do you think things will change? What is it that you really want?"

"I want my life to start and to get rid of this millstone around my neck," Annabel said, without hesitation.

The solicitor left a moment of silence for effect. "A divorce?"

"Well yes." Annabel sighed; hearing it sounded so strange. "How much does that cost? I don't really have much money."

"Well my fees will probably be between ten thousand and fifteen thousand pounds."

"Oh dear, I'm sorry, I just can't do that."

"Yes, yes of course, but you won't need to pay. We can get the fees from your husband."

"Fifteen thousand pounds?"

"Yes – plus twenty percent VAT."

"How will I live? Where will I go?" Annabel said quietly, almost to herself. Then she felt embarrassed at acting as though she were in *Gone with the Wind*.

"Mrs Farley – can I call you Annabel? – from what Marge tells me, your husband has a well-paid job, and I gather the mortgage on your home has been paid off."

"Yes."

"So, would it be possible for him to move out of the marital home and support you? Has there been any infidelity in the relationship? How bad has your husband been?"

"I don't think Mark has anyone else. I don't think he's really interested in that kind of thing!"

"So there hasn't been any infidelity?"

"No..." Annabel deliberated, "but there could be some later today." She laughed awkwardly. "I would like to start seeing people.. someone," she corrected herself. "There is a man I'd like to have a relationship with but I don't want... I don't want to do anything wrong."

"You used the word intolerable; what did you mean by that? We may be able to get you a divorce on the grounds of unreasonable behaviour. Tell me about your relationship."

"Like what? What do you mean?"

"How does he treat you?"

"Well... He is a good provider. We have two lovely children and they seem quite happy. I get to play tennis."

"Annabel, I don't mean that. I mean why are you here? What isn't working for you? What has he done or not done to make you so angry?" The solicitor gave a little sigh of frustration.

Annabel focused, thinking hard to deliver the information needed.

It took her a bit of time to get going, but after a while the momentum increased and her life of discontent, as well as Mark's shortcomings, came to light. Within a few minutes they had quite a list:

His insistence that she maintain a record of her expenditure.

Constant demands for the house to be kept tidy.

His constant need to be right.

His controlling nature.

His need to be on time.

Anal about the house work. He just wants a housekeeper

He has no friends since he is a workaholic.

Social situations, she has to be there to keep things on track, he hasn't got a clue about people's birthdays or what foods people don't like.

He is dismissive of her period pains.

All his mocking and jibing about her shopping; he wouldn't know how to buy clothes for himself and he wouldn't have a clue what people would want for Christmas presents.

His monopoly of the TV remote.
Not having an orgasm for ten years.

"OK, Annabel, thank you. Well, I've made some notes. Don't worry, I'm sure I can proceed with that."

"Great!" Annabel was glad that her thoughts could now return to Zack.

"I'd better get going with this. You don't want Mr Farley getting in first. I think we have enough to get what you need. I'll put you back on with my secretary and she will find some dates for a proper meeting."

Annabel realised that she had been having a conversation about some pretty intimate details in the middle of the street. She turned around to see if anyone she knew might have heard her.

"Mark!"

Mark was ten feet away, walking casually towards her. From his rapt expression, Annabel was pretty sure that he hadn't heard her on the phone.

"Annabel!" Mark responded, almost cheerfully.

Mark approached Annabel, and just as he had done for the last twenty years, kissed her softly on the lips.

"You're still in town – that's great! Funny thing, I decided to have a little walk too." Mark's expression became more serious. "I'm sorry if that list was insensitive. I just wanted to clear the air a bit." He smiled.

"That's OK, dear," Annabel said awkwardly, trying to reconnect with her anguish, but only finding a sense of irritation.

They stood for a moment in silence. Then Annabel felt a pair of strong arms around her. It was Zack.

"Oh God, I want you!" he said.

Annabel pushed him away and took a step back. She wanted to explain to him that Mark was there, but no words came out.

Zack followed Annabel's stare towards Mark. Mark was frozen, looking between the faces of his wife and the tennis coach.

Zack's face dropped. "You never told me you were married!"

It was a crass remark. The three of them stood there, transfixed by embarrassment. Annabel began biting her lip, taken aback at Zack's disloyalty.

Mark came to her defence. "Well, I don't think that can be quite right, can it?" He turned to face the tennis coach square on. "We have met a couple of times now." Mark fixed his eyes firmly on Zack's.

Zack folded. "Well, I'd better get going – things to do, people to see." He turned and scuttled off, nearly knocking into a rubbish bin.

Mark turned to his wife.

"Nothing's been going on," gabbled Annabel, "just some silly texts."

"That's all right, I'm sure it hasn't." Mark hesitated. "But it did look as though it was about to." Mark was unthreatening, almost affable, yet Annabel couldn't look at him.

"Mark, I think we should get a divorce," she said finally, bringing her eyes up from the floor to meet his.

"I see. Right, well, I guess that all adds up. I just needed to know." Mark cleared his throat. "Thanks." There was a pause.

"I didn't know you had someone else?"

Annabel tried to reply, but couldn't.

Mark cleared his throat. "I see I've been outmanoeuvred. I've been out of the loop, eh, darling? Perhaps I wasn't.. cut out for the job. It happens, you know: junior staff, nothing wrong with them as individuals, they just don't... suit the job.

Following on from this morning, then," he added softly, "we had some action points. I guess you don't need my holiday dates now?"

"No, dear, I don't. I've made a phone call to a solicitor already." A bus noisily passed by and Annabel waited for it to go. "I'm sorry, Mark, if this becomes difficult for you, but I just can't live the way you would like me to. It's just not me." She hesitated. "I don't think we like each other very much anymore either." Mark looked away. "My solicitor will be contacting you about it all. If you could find another place to stay, that would make things more comfortable. For both of us I think."

Mark's jaw dropped and he looked past Annabel.

"I think we've both changed over the years, Mark; things have moved on for both of us." Annabel stopped. She felt that by talking she was taking responsibility for the situation.

Mark broke the silence that followed.

"OK, darling, I understand. Time to wrap it up." He sighed heavily. "I'll wait for the paperwork and we'll go from there. Thanks for everything." He paused and then found a good solid point to finish. "It didn't end well, but there were some good times."

"Yes, dear." Annabel felt her anger now completely dissipated, and replaced by her pity for Mark. "Bye." And without knowing where she was going, she stepped away.

Mark continued, "I mean *all* the good times, and there were many!"

Annabel stepped back towards him, her mouth open.

"The boys!" Mark smiled. "Tim with his wonderful sense of fun; he's a handsome boy. Simon and his infectious laughter." Mark broadened his smile. "He's going to be very successful in whatever career he chooses. All from us."

Annabel moved to interrupt him but Mark continued. "And then of course there are all those wonderful years we had together before the kids, all those dinner parties and the entertaining. We were so good together. Hey, and don't forget those amazing holidays; learning to ski together, that was such a laugh!" Mark smiled at her.

"Oh, Mark!" Annabel filled the silence. "You and your lists!"

Mark's smile dropped. Annabel saw his face change and wanted to assure him she had said it with affection. She liked his desire for the moment to end well.

"And you can add to that list," she continued, "the night we made Tim. In fact, that whole holiday in Paris; that was magical." She paused, waiting for Mark to register her approval. "You made our Christmases so special – you were a great Father Christmas." She gave Mark the biggest, most genuine smile she could muster. "Goodbye, Mark," she whispered, and left.

Chapter Three

Mark meandered amongst the oncoming pedestrians, lost in thought. He had gone to work with the object of resolving some issues with his marriage; it never occurred to him that his marriage would end up over. It really didn't seem real, and all before lunchtime! Had it all changed that morning, or had he simply woken up to what was already there?

Now he had a whole *new* list of issues to deal with. In just a few footsteps, the repercussions of the morning's events hit him, like a machine gun spraying out bullets.

Where would he live? When would he see the children? Who would end up with the record collection? (They had both added to it over the years but it was he who continued to play them). Would he take some of the furniture? He would be expected to go out and get new stuff; perhaps she would help him with that?

What would the guys at work say? It would be embarrassing. What would his mother say? 'I told you so', probably.

It seemed inevitable that she would move on and find a new man. But the tennis coach was not in her league. He smiled to himself as he realised that he would want to vet the men she might meet in order to protect her. He couldn't help wanting the best for her.

He recalled her list of good times. Once upon a time, she had fancied him. Once upon a time, he had made her happy. What had changed? And could it be changed back?

She'd put Paris on her list of highlights. Now that really *did* feel like a different person's life. What was she thinking of, with his long hair and his big ego? He had danced on the table at the restaurant and flirted with the *maître d'*, flirted with everyone, yet somehow never made Annabel the slightest bit anxious. Perhaps now he wasn't so carefree? They had skipped down the streets of Paris, making friends with complete strangers! Partying hard, yet somehow still having energy when they got back to the bedroom. And then the morning! Breakfast in bed was complete carnage for the fine bed linen. To have shown such disregard for the perfection of that luxurious Louis XV carved bed, and how they had made no attempt to tidy up! Definitely a different Mark. But perhaps a Mark who hadn't found his priorities in life?

He saw the park bench was free and decided to sit for a while. As he watched the children play he considered what had happened. He'd got through stuff like this before, where he'd judged a situation without the right regard or consideration to the other party. It was easy to do when you were leading a team and under pressure; sometimes someone just had to make a decision and go forward. When it all went wrong and he'd got the signal that he'd messed up, it was time to make his apologies, explain the confusion and try and reach some compromise. At work, there were always negotiations that could be made. Even when he received the most negative of criticisms, there were always things that could be done. When the new sales manager had threatened to resign over his move to a new branch, they had agreed a relocation package. When their major client had shown signs that they would test out what their competitor could provide, they had put together a presentation showing what their future plans were to enhance their service. There was always something that could be done. So what was needed here? Where would he go to reach a compromise? ACAS?

Mark's phone vibrated, shouting at him for attention. It was Janice at the office.

"Mark, I've been trying to contact you!" Mark looked at his phone and saw the long list of missed calls and texts. He'd been oblivious to them. "Are you all right? You've missed a load of meetings."

"Something's come up." Mark struggled to find a plausible excuse. "It's... well, quite awful really. It's a personal matter." He swallowed. "That is, a friend's personal matter."

"A personal matter? What kind of personal matter?"

"Well... It's to do with his wife. He tried to have a talk with her about her behaviour and it's all gone horribly wrong. Within an hour she's approached a solicitor for a divorce! I think I might get him to go to ACAS."

"ACAS? I would have thought Relate was more relevant."

Mark paused, not wanting to appear ignorant. "What do they do? What does 'RELATE' stand for?"

Janice paused. "Relate, as in 'relationship'!"

Mark realised that he was sounding stupid but he really needed to know. Could he risk one more question?

"What do they do?"

"Marriage guidance, Mark!"

"Well yes, I had thought of them." He immediately felt foolish for trying to cover his lack of knowledge. The stress of the day was showing its impact on his resilience. He sighed heavily. *Damn, she would have heard that.* He hated it when the junior knew more than he did. He spent most of his career ensuring that didn't happen.

"Shall I text you their number?" She hesitated. "For your friend, I mean?"

"I don't know. She seemed pretty determined." Mark realised that he sounded miserable and reflected that that was pretty much how he felt – plus hopeless and desperate.

"Perhaps she could be persuaded to consider it. Perhaps she just needs to hear the words, 'I love you'?"

There was silence. Mark felt like a rabbit staring at approaching headlights.

"Look, try this, send two texts..." She paused. "No, make that four. First say, 'I still love you, I don't know how to show that sometimes. Sorry.' Then say, 'I still want you', and say something sexy."

"Sexy? Like what?"

Mark heard Janice's frustrated tut.

"I think that could be something your friend can think of, but if he's really struggling it could be something like, 'I still want you, you're gorgeous, especially in that black dress you wore last night'."

"What black dress?"

"Mark! You'll have to use your imagination."

"Right, yes. And then what?"

"Then, the next text is, 'Will you give us a chance?' Then, finally, just a text saying, 'Would you come to Relate with me?' Ooh and don't forget the text hug!"

"A text hug?"

"Open brackets, space, closed brackets."

"Couldn't I..., er, *he* just call her?"

"Well no; he's tried that. Talking isn't working right now. That's the point, Mark, isn't it!?"

"OK, OK. Why four separate texts? Isn't it clearer if I do one?"

"Mark! Are you writing a business letter or getting your wife... your *friend's* wife... back?"

*

Annabel had returned to the coffee bar and was nursing her latte. She was trying to calm down. She had decided to try and think about something completely different to the morning's events, but thoughts kept popping into her mind, uninvited.

She couldn't help but feel disloyal. She was angry at the solicitor for so rapidly suggesting a divorce. Was there a bit of self-interest there? How about fifteen thousand pounds' worth of self-interest! And what was Marge doing telling the solicitor all about her life as though she knew better?

When Mark had challenged Zack she'd recognised what she'd been attracted to when he was younger. Quiet, but strong, and choosing his words carefully. *Pretty effective this time*, she thought; *he saw him off faster than a Roddick ace*.

A text came.

She didn't look at it. *It'll be Zack*, she thought, *how pathetic!* She felt completely let down by him. OK, it was awkward, but his first response was to dismiss her. *Spineless prat!*

The phone chirped again, but she was even more determined not to look at it.

She sat back and enjoyed the final part of her latte. Then in one mouthful she devoured half of her chocolate muffin, oblivious to its taste.

The phone chirped again. Perhaps it was from the kids?

Perhaps Mark had gone and done something stupid?

She grabbed at the phone. The texts were from Mark.

'I still love you, I don't know how to show that sometimes. Sorry.'

'I still want you, you're still that gorgeous girl with the perfect smile and wonderful giggle in Paris. I wish we were still there in that funny restaurant on the Ile St Louis.'

'Will you give us a chance?'

Her mouth fell open. *How sweet*, she thought. Then, as she held the phone, the last text arrived.

'Would you come to Relate with me? ( )'

Relate! She hadn't seen that coming.
She read his second text again.
Annabel looked up. Her mind went straight back to that night when Mark had had the whole restaurant singing 'When the Saints Go Marching In'. They had been rewarded with a free bottle of champagne. How has it gone from that to Relate?
She knew that she must think carefully before replying, but within a second her finger hovered over the keypad: 'O' and then 'K', and then, just before she sent it, an 'x'.

Mark looked at the kiss on his phone. His thumb rubbed the 'x' on the screen. It was the first text kiss he had received from her. A little bit of Mark wanted to file the text away, it was an important document. But the part of him that had grown that day, enjoyed the moment for what it was.

As he walked back to his car, he planned the next step in his campaign. The spring in his step returned, not perhaps with the same vigour as the morning, but it was there all the same.

About the Author

Luke McEwen was born in Chichester, West Sussex, UK in 1964, the second son of Andrew and Anitra McEwen. His father was a journalist for the Daily Mail for twenty six years, finally ending that career as chief diplomatic correspondent to the Financial Times. Luke spent four years of his childhood in Freeport, New York, and eighteen months in Brussels, where he attended the Common Market School. He finally returned to his home town nine years later in 1973. Luke went to the University of East Anglia and studied Politics and Sociology. Just to avoid any confusion, he sadly did not attend the UEA's famous writing course. But did attend Chichester College's creative writing course led by Julia Homan. Luke continues to work and live in Chichester with his son. He is a keen potter and painter, tennis and saxophone player.

He has a blog and writer's website at www.lukemcewen.co.uk

Printed in Great Britain
by Amazon